CARNIVAL OF HORRORS:
The (IM) Perfect Vacation!

AF080829

Orangebooks Publication

1st Floor, Rajhans Arcade, Mall Road, Kohka, Bhilai, Chhattisgarh 490020

Website: **www.orangebooks.in**

© Copyright, 2024, Author

All rights reserved. No part of this book may be reproduced, stored in a retrieval system, or transmitted, in any form by any means, electronic, mechanical, magnetic, optical, chemical, manual, photocopying, recording or otherwise, without the prior written consent of its writer.

First Edition, 2024
ISBN: 978-93-6554-152-6

CARNIVAL OF HORRORS
THE (IM) PERFECT VACATION

RUDVED PALSOKAR

OrangeBooks Publication
www.orangebooks.in

PROLOGUE

CHAPTER 0

"This creation of mine is going to be the best I have ever created. It will rule over the world greater than any of my creations have or better than I have myself!" The mysterious wizard exclaimed. He glued a few wooden parts on his creation and put a voice modulator inside which was enchanted by his own dark magic. For the dummy to be awaken, the wizard wrote a few words on a piece of paper, which was, of course, enchanted by his dark magic, and read it in his raspy voice. The dummy woke up and slapped his creator smack right on the face" Why'd you do that?" The wizard cried, rubbing his cheek with his hand in a gentle way to stop the pain." I'm sorry, but you only made me this way. So, your loss." The dummy said in the same scratchy voice the wizard spoke in when he woke the dummy up, almost as if he wasn't sorry at all." It's okay, as long as you help me in my plan." The wizard said, staring into the black, dark eyes of the dummy. "What is it? Speak up fast, unless you want to become some shark food." The dummy said, showing his hook to his creator in a fierceful manner." Okay, okay. No need to get tempered, even though you are." The wizard smirked." First, before you tell me anything. Tell me what my name is!" The dummy declared." How do you like the name… Fantôme!" The wizard exclaimed, as if he was naming a priceless art." Hmmm…I guess it's okay. But what does it mean?" The dummy said in an unsure voice. The wizard really didn't want to deal with this, so he ignored the question." Okay then, Fantôme, how would you like to wreak havoc all over the world!" The wizard said, as if he was about to tell an evil plan. Fantôme liked the sound of it, so he agreed." I will be honoured to!" Fantôme said in an agreement manner." But wait, why don't we start with something small. Perhaps a family ?!" said the mysterious wizard. The dummy agreed. "Okay then, let's start NOW Fantôme!" The wizard said, then started to laugh maliciously. Thinking this was evil, Fantôme started doing it along with his master! MWA-HA-HA-HA-HA-HA!

CONTENT

Part I

The Beginning

Chapter 1.. 2

Chapter 2.. 7

Chapter 3..12

Chapter 4 18

Chapter 5..28

Chapter 6 40

Chapter 7..50

Part II

The Twist

Chapter 8 62

Chapter 9 74

Chapter 10.. 84

Chapter 11..99

Chapter 12 110

PART I

THE BEGINNING

CHAPTER 1

Matt and I were just about to enter Horrorpark. My name is Lizy Morris and I am 14 years old. My younger brother, Matt, is 11 years old. He has been so excited about this trip that he's stopped bugging me for, like, a week! He was thrilled to get "spooked up" by horror park! We parked our Caravan in the parking lot and got carried to our hotel by a mini-train ride! We went to the ticket booth to get our hotel keys. There was nobody, except a shadowy figure in the booth." Ummm . . . excuse me, sir?" said my dad, in a nervous and sweat-breaking way. Then we saw an ugly creature, he roared in a ferocious voice and then we all screamed, at the top of our lungs, with him! When we all stopped screaming, my dad asked the ticketer" Who the heck are you?". The ticketer said he was a "horror" and said that his job was to frighten any new guests who come in." Anyhow, you have a free stay here for . . . 2 weeks, am I right, Mr. Morris?" said the horror." Yes!" my father replied, instantly. The horror introduced himself to us, and he said his name is Tyson and he gave us two key cards for the rooms. Our room was on the 20th floor, which was on the rooftop." Isn't that neat!" I said. We took the elevator, and you won't believe how fast we went up! We went into our rooms and kept our bags in. Matt reached the bathroom first to freshen up, which left me to keep the bags in. When I opened the closet to keep my clothes, I saw a dummy dressed up like a pirate. He had wavy hair, which was a combination of brown and grey. He had a pirate hat with a skull on it. He had a hook on one of his hands. And, he was wearing black pants with a black belt and a golden buckle attached to it. Attached to him was a note. I took the note and unfolded it.

"My name is Fantôme, I am a ventriloquist dummy.".

Below the note was another message, which was in an extremely smaller font than the other words. I read the other message" Flip this note around". I had already checked, and there was nothing on the other side of the piece of paper. But, hesitantly, I flipped the note. Magically, or so, some words appeared on the other side of the piece of paper.

The words on the other side were weird words which I didn't understand. "Let me see, too." Matt said, coming out of the washroom. He might be a small kid, but he has got some serious observing skills at some times. For a second, I seriously forgot that he was there, too. He tried to snatch the note from me, but I was faster than him." NOLI ME TURBARE,

PHANTASMA!" I read. Instantly, the dummy woke up and pointed at us and said," Finally, after a century of sleeping, I have woken up. Now I will punish the whole world by destroying it. And don't worry, you will witness it with me, my servants". Matt and I didn't know what to do, we were too scared. And we also wanted to get one point cleared. We were no servants of anyone. We didn't even try to attack him, because from the fact that he's been living for a century, he is no guy to be messing with. So, we ran to the elevator and went to the reception. Luckily, there was someone at the desk. We went to him. The receptionist said his name was Larry. I fidgeted with my fingers, "Larry, There is some weird ventriloquist dummy named Fantôme in our room closet." I said to him in a scared voice." Really? I don't think so. Because we don't have any ventriloquist dummies, especially one named Fantôme!" Larry said to us in a confirmed and determined voice." Can you just come to our room to check." Matt jumped in. "Sure, I see no problem in that. "Larry said, while walking with us towards the elevator. He pressed the button of the 20th floor and we went up. Once we reached, we went inside the room. Matt and I were expecting to see Fantôme inside the closet, but he wasn't there. Instead, he was gone. "What, I don't understand. He was right here!" Matt said, searching all over the room. Suddenly I remembered that we haven't seen our parents for a long time." Hey, where are Mom & Dad?" I said. Matt didn't remember, either. So, we rushed to Larry, instantly. He said" Are you talking about Mr.& Mrs. Morris. Oh right, they went outside. They left about a few moments ago. Surprisingly, they were in a hurry. And I forgot to mention that they were also carrying a dummy in their arms.". Matt and I couldn't believe what we heard. That our parents left. That also, with Fantôme instead of us! There was some problem going on. I could sense it. Because I know my parents, and they always put us ahead of everyone, even themselves. We had to find out what happened to them. Did they actually leave without us? Or did someone forcefully make them leave the hotel, leaving us behind? Well, that was an extra mystery which we had to solve!

CHAPTER 2

1 ½ WEEK AGO...

Matt and I were just arriving from school. The mailman was dropping a message in our mailbox. It was mid-afternoon, around 3:00 PM. When the mailman disappeared, we went to check the mail. On our way there, we saw the all time neighbourhood lover – Abby Summer." Hey Abby, what are you doing here right now?" I asked, curiously." Oh nothing, just came to receive the mail. What about you?" she asked." We just came from school and were just about to take the mail, too." Matt said before I could say anything, taking out the mail from the mailbox." Well, looks like we've got to go now, right Matt !"I said loudly so that Abby could hear me clearly, while elbowing him in his side-ribs. He nodded and we went home." I really get scared in front of that Abby girl. She hits me with that withering - eye look!" He shivered once we went inside. I ignored him and just kept my bag under the dining table.

"Mom. Dad. Look, the mailman dropped this letter in our mailbox." I yelled across the house. Mom and Dad suddenly appeared, both on their laptops. They both worked, so that left me to do most of the chores as Matt won't do much. My mothers name is Anna morris, and my dads name is Gabriel Morris. My mother is 40 years old, while my dad is 45 years old. I showed the letter to dad and he ripped it open." Oh wow, would you look at that. We've got a special invitation to "Horrorpark" below the downtown city, like… somewhere in a jungle." dad said, squinting his eyes. The address was as if it was supposed to be hidden. Dad searched the place up on google maps, but the location was unknown. There was a link on the invitation, and dad searched it up. He got the location, but it was from a different website. Dad ignored it." It just opened and looks like we're one of the special guests there", he said with a bright smile on his face." Let me see". mom declared, grabbing the invitation from dads hands." Pretty impressive" mom said" Oh, that means we got a free vacation. Time to party, guys. We'll have to go shopping and do all the packing, and oh goodness we have plenty of things to do. When are we going?" Mom said, rapidly. Mom is a shopping-freak, so if you want to take advice from someone about a vacation, mom's the one to speak to." The invitation says we are invited on the 11th of june."I popped up before dad could answer.

"Splendid, hey don't your school vacations start from the 5th of june. And todays just the 2nd. Your school vacations start after a couple of days school, now isn't that fun for you!" Mom said, with a gleam in her eye and a bright smile on her face. Matt and I nodded and headed towards our room." I'm not sure I like this horrorpark thing. But hey, it is just a week away. No problem in that." Matt said, taking a bite out of his apple and searching something on the web." What are you searching on the web?" I asked, with curiosity in my mind." Some information about horrorpark. It says here that the information hasn't officially come up yet. Since it opened a week ago, the manager is refusing to give any information." Matt said, still looking up things on the web. "Are you sure about this? I mean, like, come on. Some random letter comes up to us and says 'Hey, you're invited to our grand hotel. Please come up here and take no information about us.' It's just so shady. And how do they even know about us, anyway!" I said in a fit of rage.

"I have no idea, but all I know is that we got a free vacation!"

"Fine, let's start packing. I think I'm gonna love this FREE trip anyways."

We started packing for this "so-called free trip".

***

1 WEEK AGO...

We have just started packing our bags and suitcases. We're taking the stuff most people would take to an average resort. We're not taking too much because we think that we'll get most of the necessary items there, such as shampoos, conditioners, shower caps, etc." But I want to take my Hot Wheels race track set." Matt kept insisting. He loved cars." No, there's going to be plenty of amusement there." Mom kept saying to Matt. I just sat there and watched the drama. Matt was thinking about sneaking some of his cars in, but he got busted by dad accidentally." This is gonna be the most grand trip in the history of epic trips!" Matt exclaimed." Yeah, yeah. I think you mean 'most EPIC trip in history of epic trips!'. "I said sarcastically, rolling my eyes. Matt growled at me "Mom can you tell Lizy to please stop correcting me in grammar cause she's a nerd!". Mom yelled "We still love your good grades, so don't stop your grades but stop annoying your brother. Please!", while carrying the suitcases to the car. "Too bad that you're not as excited as me." Matt said" It's actually not your fault, god just made you that way. I mean, if you don't want to come on this trip, just say so. "Matt said, trying to make me mad." If you want my fist to land on your mouth, just say so!" I said in a fit of rage." Jeez, now would you look at that. You really have a short temper, sis." Matt said, in a reaction as if he just got shocked by an electric eel, then he started laughing like a clown. Not to mention that he is one. He's like a person who's mood-swings even god himself can't figure out." Ugh... I wish the trip was today itself!" Matt groaned, as if he's being tortured in his mind." What are you thinking about right now?" I asked Matt, thinking that he'd be thinking how the video games he plays were invented. He does that sometimes, we think it's weird but he says it's cool! And to give you an idea of what he plays, he plays Earthbound, the weirdest game in our whole freaking city!" Nah" he finally said" I'm thinking about the things which could be there at the resort." He said in a hurried voice. "Well, we're going there in a week, so you could check it out later." I said to him. Well, little did Matt know that he'd regret his choice.

CHAPTER 3

PRESENT DAY

First of all, the library was huge! We didn't even know where to start looking. It's almost been an hour since we came in here to search for a book to stop Fantôme, yet, we've found nothing so far. We thought that there must be some book at least about ventriloquist dummies (Who weren't magical). But, sadly, there were none! Matt and I thought of an idea, and we raced to our parents' room. We thought that since they are missing, they must have left some clue for us. We searched their whole room, yet, we found nothing. Just when we were about to leave, we heard something beeping. It was coming from their closet, which was half opened. I saw dads GOPRO camera, which I had gifted to him on his 40th birthday. It was blinking red, that meant it was still recording. If it had been blinking green, then, that meant it was done recording. I turned the recording off, and watched the tape. It showed that our parents were being pulled out to the door. Then we saw Fantôme, once they were gone. Suddenly, the lights went off. And when they came back on, Fantôme had disappeared. That means he, really, did want to get revenge on the whole world. And he started with our parents!

Matt and I were pacing around the room, thinking about where our parents could be. We thought that Fantôme couldn't have gone too far! Maybe just around the hotel, or somewhere. "He could've gone to the cafe beside our resort." Matt suggested. He could never think of anything besides food! Yet, 10 minutes later I found myself at the cafe beside their resort, 'The haunted haven'. They had paper ghosts hanging outside the cafe, and a fake zombie at the entrance, who was trying to scare us, but had failed multiple times! And, instead of being scared, we laughed! We felt that all of this was strange with all the coincidences, like first Fantôme and then the strange cafe beside our resort, that we both thought that we were in a nightmare.

But eventually we made our mind and, we went inside the cafe with fear that we wouldn't see our parents again, and saw people dressed in weird shaped costumes. For a second or so, we forgot that it was just a normal sunday, not Halloween. There was a long table in the cafe. There were songs going on, and everybody was having fun! We asked, whoever we could, if they had seen our parents come into this cafe. None of them knew. "Probably because of the racket going on in here," said Matt. "How will we ever find our parents?" I said, miserably." It was my fault that Fantôme woke up, and kidnapped our parents." I said. "I don't know if this was your fault or mine. But, what I do know, is that we have to find our parents. FAST!" Matt replied to me. We went from shops to shops, streets to streets & from alleys to alleys putting posters of our parents which we printed. We also kept my phone number below the pictures of our missing parents. "We're never gonna find our parents. "said Matt, with only one poster of our parents in his hand. I was about to say something, but, I got a call from an unknown number. I picked up the call, and said "Hello, who is this?", confused. The person on the other side replied to me "Hello, my name is Carlos, I saw a poster of your parents. For a second, I was like 'They seem familiar to me, right?' and then I remembered that I had seen them, just a few moments ago, in a cafe called 'Haunted Haven'. I'm following them right now. I'll send you my coordinates in a second". Instantly, his coordinates showed up on my phone.

***

I started looking up his coordinates, he was up at the alley right beside haunted haven. We went there as fast as we could, reaching in about a minute or so. When we reached there, we didn't see our parents. Surprisingly, a weird teenager waved at us, almost as if he was calling us. "That MUST be Carlos. "I whispered to Matt, approaching Carlos. We went to him. He was dressed like one of those typical teenage boys, who probably had lots of friends but no one is bothered about his where abouts. He was wearing a red cap a purple basketball shirt which said 'Go Beavers!'(Which probably indicated that he was either on a basketball team, or was a fan of that team). I didn't see how I thought about him like that, but I just got the image in my head. I really didn't like criticising people, but it probably didn't matter because nobody heard it but me because I said it in my head. Plus, we learnt not to 'Judge A Book By It's Cover'.

Before we could say anything, he said "I saw the dummy in your parents' hands. He, like, woke up and started saying some weird words. Then, the wall just tore open and, they went inside. I tried to go inside the wall with them, but the wall closed instantly after they went in!" He finished panting." That creep is using our parents as slaves. We've got to stop him!" said Matt, in a panic." We will, sooner or later after we save our parents, we'll get our revenge on him." I said, to cheer him up a bit. When my brother panics, he is not able to do anything. So, I better let him know that everything is okay. Even when it is not.

We waited for hours and hours for Mom & Dad to reappear. But we saw nobody come out of the wall. "What if they never come back. What if Fantôme's held them hostage, and he'll never return them to us?" said Matt." Or, it is possible that, they could've gone from the other side of the wall?" Carlos said, with a sweat-breaking face. Matt and I, both, scowled at him." HOW COULD YOU NOT TELL US THIS BEFORE?!" We both yelled at him, in anger." Well, I thought that since they went through here, they would come through here, too." Carlos said. Matt and I, ignoring him, ran to the other side of the wall instantly. Carlos was following us, trying not to be seen, but failing so badly. Probably because we're both so mad at him! We reached to the other side of the wall, exhausted. We were all expecting that Fantôme would come out of the wall any second along with our parents, but … no. Nothing happened.

"They must have come out of there sooner." I said to Matt and Carlos." Well it's pretty late, don't you think guys? We should all get some sleep now." said Carlos.

CHAPTER 4

Matt and I, slowly, walked to our hotel. We both kept observing the other streets, alleys, shops and walls. Especially the walls. As soon as we reached the hotel, we searched for Larry. But we couldn't see him, anywhere. Which was very odd, because we never saw him get out of the hotel. We went to our parent's room, and, everything there was normal. But then, suddenly, we saw a shadowy figure move. We went to the front desk, again, to see if Larry was there. This time he was there, surprisingly." Hey Larry, where were you a few minutes ago? We came here but you were gone." I said to him, observing him thoroughly." YAA." said my brother, trying to look like one of the investigators in his cop-like movies." Well…I was cleaning your room. It was messy, so I thought that 'Hey, since they're so special guests, I might as well clean their room while they're gone so they wouldn't be disturbed later!'" said Larry, as if he was hiding something.

I wasn't so sure if he was saying the truth, but I didn't have any evidence that he was lying, too." Okay, thanks." I said to Larry. We headed towards the lift. Once we went inside, I said to Matt" Larry is acting very…suspiciously-weird, right? Anyways, who cleans the room on the same day of checking.". There had to be some connection between the disappearance between our parents and Larry. I opened the room with my key card, and all of our stuff was…gone! I couldn't believe it. I rubbed my eyes to see if I was imagining it, but, no. all our belongings were actually gone! I looked at Matt, and he was acting as if his eyes had popped out." Oh no…Where is all of our stuff?!" he said, panicking, then he went into his action-movie face and said". Uhmmm ... I mean, Someone must have stolen our belongings.". I was panicking a lot since all of our stuff was gone, and I didn't know what to do! I guessed it must have been Larry. Because, he was the last one in our room. I rushed to the reception to chew him out. But once again, he was gone like superman! I didn't know where to find him.

So, I went out of the hotel. I was in plenty of panic right now. I forgot to think about the cars speeding on the street. For a second or so, I was in my own world, thinking how much worse could this day be for me. And just after that thought, a car almost crashed into me! I was frozen once the man in the car squealed the brakes on me. He came out of the car and apologised to me immediately. He said he was sorry, as he wasn't paying attention on the road. Just when I was about to say something to the man, Matt came, running and puffing. He said "How many times have I told you not to run without me!?". He did not see the man in front of me. I, literally, had to signal him with my eyes that the man was in front of me. When Matt did see the man, the man asked us" Are you both siblings? Because you look very alike!". Matt said" Yes! We both are siblings, how did you know?". Sometimes, my brother acts as if he's the dumbest person on the planet, even if the answer is right in front of him. I'll bet you 20 bucks that he wouldn't even know if I got cut by a knife even if it happened right in front of him. I don't know if he does that on purpose or what, but, I should really start considering with mom and dad to keep him in a mental hospital to get checked after this vacation! I mean like, come on, what is wrong with that boy." He just said that we look alike. Therefore, we're siblings!" I said to him. He looked at me, dumbfounded. He's so stupid, that I left him there, mouth opened and eyes popped out.

We went ahead, without the man who said his name was Alexander. Again, Matt followed me by running. I feel that this day was very weird, because we're meeting new people every minute! Honestly, I just wanted this day to end. But, this day feels like it is never-ending! And by looking at Matt's face, I think he feels the same as me, too. I just wanted to go home, and, sleep on my bed. I'll listen to songs, go to parks with my parents. But, no! This day is even worse than my 11th birthday, when Matt punched me in my face at my birthday party and I cried for a very long time. Anyways, I have to focus on my mission. This mission is life or death for my parents, so I have to hurry. Just as me and Matt were about to creep up the wall to find if there is another portal, something growled. It growled as if it was hungry. Suddenly, the growling became louder and louder as we went closer to the wall. Then, I noticed it was coming from me and Matt's stomach's. We were both exhausted from the mystery solving, and we needed a break. We both started searching for a place to eat. Eventually, we found a place to eat. The place was old, dusty and had cobwebs on the doors and windows. It felt as if it wasn't opened for ages, but lights were on inside and…it looked as if people were partying inside!" So weird! They even have fake spiders on their roof, what big creeps, right?" Matt said." Yeah." I replied to Matt, distracted. We went in the ' Ghostly Gatherings', slowly and carefully. When we went inside everybody were partying and dancing. Suddenly, I fell to the ground, feeling sleepy." Sis? Sis, wake up!" Matt said, continuously. But I didn't wake up. Instead, I started having a dream.

***

The dream started something like this. I was in a dark and hollow room. Suddenly, I heard a raspy voice." Fantôme!" I said to myself. The voice was coming from behind the walls. I went beyond the walls, to the voices. There was a board. It read "Welcome to the 'secret hideout'!". Okay, at this point, I was totally scared. Literally, like that scared-out cat in the little junior horror books. I went inside the room, and it was humongous. I couldn't believe that they called this a room. If I were the owner, I would call it a mansion! Anyways, I had to focus on finding my parents. I searched everywhere, but I couldn't find a single clue. In fact, the only clue I got was the trembling of my tiring legs. Suddenly, as I was in the study room, I saw a magnifying glass. I took it, and pointed it at the floor. The thing I found which was weird, was that I found some footprints. "They must be moms & dads! "I said, with excitement. But wait, there was another set of footprints, they were very small. Fantôme's'! Saying his name, I got a bitter taste in my mouth. Time to get revenge on him. I went inside the secret door. Thinking how many wicked and vile things lie beyond this 'secret door'!

Once I was in the secret door, I heard voices. One was as if it was innocent, but still being punished. It was mom's. Then, I heard another voice. This time it was an evil and raspy voice. I recognized it immediately. Who else's voice could be that evil and raspy other than the prince of evil, Fantôme! Oh, how much I wanted to get revenge on that ugly, little creep! But, I had to remain silent. The place was very dusty, and I'm allergic to dust. But this is just a dream, so nothing will happen I thought. But no, I did cough. And then, Fantôme heard me. He turned his head and I heard dad's voice "Run Lizy! Find us later. We will-". "Ahh, shut your mouth." Fantôme interfered." Now listen, dear Lizy, if you want to see your parents alive, you better not try to stop me. Or else they'll be long gone from you, longer than you realise your brain is from your head. MWAHAHAHA." He said, ending with an evil laugh. How could he laugh at a time like this. OH no, I have to do something, or my parents would be gone forever. Infuriated, I ran to Fantôme to strangle him. But, as soon as I touched him, he disappeared.

I was back in the real world, on my bed in the hotel room. "It was a vision!" I said to myself. "What was a vision?" somebody said, approaching the room. The light was dim and the person also got dimmed in the light. I squinted my eyes and recognized who it was.

It was Matt! I was so happy to see him, that I almost got up to hug him. "It's okay, you need to get some rest. "Matt said, putting a cold cloth over my forehead. "What happened?!" I said, surprised and shocked. "We were in the ghostly gatherings restaurant, and you collapsed to the ground. I carried you to the room here, and I called the nurse. She said that you were fine, and that you collapsed to the ground due to hypertension. "Matt said to me, while putting the cloth in the glass of cold water and back on my forehead. "Well, thanks but I'm feeling better now. Now we've got to continue the search for mom and dad" I said, trying to get up from my bed. "You're not going anywhere!" Matt said, with a caring expression on his face. "But we have to find Mom & Dad!" I said in a loud voice." I'll go alone, with Carlos.

I texted him, and, he said he'll meet me at 9:30. he said, showing me the text and about to leave the room. I was about to protest, but I knew he was doing this all just to keep me safe. So, I sucked all the words right in my mouth. He left the room, instructing the nurse to take good care of me. The nurse said to me "Do you want something to drink or eat? Perhaps, if you want, you can watch the T.V or play board games. If you want anything, just ring the bell.", pointing to the rope beside my bed. Then, she left the room. I thought about my parents. I thought about my brother in a fretful way. What Fantôme wanted was very unclear! Couldn't he just tell us the moment he went! I understood he wanted revenge, but in what way?

***

Matt and Carlos started roaming the alleys, to find the place I described in my dream. "What do you have in mind?" said Carlos to Matt, kinda looking bored. "I'm worried about my sister! I know the nurses are taking good care of her, but I feel like I should be there for her. She has too many things to worry about, and I don't want to be in one of those parts of her mind!. "Matt replied to Carlos. He didn't say anything after that, so Matt just kept shut. They finally found the place, like after a millennia! At least, they thought they did. It was pretty similar looking to the place in my dream. There was a weird hole in the alley wall which looked like a portal. Matt put his hand through it to check if it was just a drawing. But, it surprised him as it was not." Woah! That's cool. "Matt said, Carlos replied to him by saying" Magnificent" in a French accent, and putting his hands in a scrunched up manner like he saw in that 'Habibi' meme. "The accent was cool, but don't ever do that again. It gives me the chills!" Matt said to him. They went through the portal drawing (or illusion portal, as Carlos would say), to solve my dream mystery. '*I mean, how hard could it be?*' Matt thought.

1 HOUR LATER . . .

So far, it's been a nightmare finding something, or someone here. Matt and Carlos have been stuck in this stupid door for almost an hour or so, trying to find the answer to this riddle. They had to solve a riddle to go through the door. Fantôme sure covered up his tracks well. The riddle was" I haunt you and scare you. You can't see me, but I will always see you at the darkest hour! Who am I?". "A heck of a riddle it is, for sure" said Carlos. Instead of replying to him, Matt started thinking of answers. But, all his guesses were useless. "I wish they would've given us some type of clue!" Matt said, And almost instantly, a note in his hand. It said 18th August…. That was a totally useless hint. Then, after a few moments later, Matt got the answer. Once, we went to grandma's house and she told us that on 18 august it was ghost day. We didn't believe her, but surely, the next day there were…" Ghosts!" Matt screamed, with happiness. The stone door started with a Crumbling, then it changed to a grumbling and finally it opened with a rumbling. They went inside the stone door, and they were shocked to see who it was. Our nightmare was standing in front of their eyes. It was…

CHAPTER 5

Fantôme! Standing in between our parents." Hand over our parents, dummy. Or you're going to pay for it." Matt said." Pay for it ? I hardly think that I'm going to 'Pay for it', you imbeciles. I have your parents kidnapped, I am the one with power, I am the king!" Fantôme laughed aloud. Matt was shocked, but not surprised. He knew that Fantôme was evil, but he was going to stop him. Matt scanned his surroundings for anything. He found a lever at the end of the right side corner of the room. Matt dashed to it and pushed it down. Fantôme wasn't fast enough. A cage dropped upon him and he got startled. He dropped the remote in his hand, and Matt picked it up. Before he could press the red button, Carlos called out to him." Your parents aren't here, it was an illusion !".Matt screamed furiously, and pressed the red button. Suddenly, the cupboard opened and mom and dad came out. But, they weren't Matt's' parents, but they were robots of their parents' duplicates.

Matt recognized immediately. Because if they really were, they would've freaked out after being trapped in a cupboard for… let's just say, a long time. Carlos went over to the robots as soon as he saw matt eye signal to fight them. He told Fantôme that if he didn't show him where his parents were he was going to burn this place down. Fantôme refused to tell. But Matt saw another remote in his pocket. And he got an idea. He said to Fantôme "Well, I guess you win. So would you just tell us about how to open this cage."Fantôme was flabbergasted, by the look on his face. And so was Carlos. Even the robots attacking Carlos stopped for a second. Carlos was trying to think out what Matt was talking about, but before he could even speak, Fantôme spoke up." Yes yes. It's the button behind the cupboard where your 'fake parents' were trapped. But hey, you're not gonna attack me once I come come out, right." Fantôme winced at the last sentence in a tiny voice.

Matt and Carlos almost started to feel sorry for him, even the robots did. But if there's anything Matt has learned from his bad cop-good cop movies, it's that never trust our opponents. No mercy! He gave a sign to Carlos and he led the robots to the button. He jumped on the wall and boomeranged over the robots. The robots crashed over each other, and then they got circuited. One of them smashed the button, of the cage. Once the cage lifted, Carlos held up Fantôme by his collar and Matt said to him "Now tell us our parents' location, creep!". Fantôme tried to make up an excuse, but they could see through him. He eventually told us that they were inside a secret room, and they asked him to take them there. We dragged him to any wall we could see, any hidden place, literally anything. We finally found it and we opened a secret door in a closet. My parents fell to the ground and gasped for air." Thank you, young man, for saving us. May I know your name please?" My dad said, acting as if he owed his life to Carlos. Matt and I always call him the 'Drama King' at home, for these type of reactions." The name is Windward, CARLOS Windward, Sir." said Carlos, trying to impress my dad even more. What a show-off he is." Where is Lizy?" my dad asked Matt." She's in the hotel health room. She's fine, just that her blood pressure was too high, so she fainted. The nurse is taking care of her." Matt replied. Just as they were leaving, Fantôme caught Matt's leg and Matt cried." Not on my watch, you stupid dummy!" he said." Leave me alone!" Matt screamed in tension. Suddenly, something kicked Fantôme on the head. It was Carlos! What perfect timing he had come on." BEGONE, YOU STUPID DUMMY!" he said. Fantôme fell backwards, and They went out of the wall. The portal was just closing behind them, when they heard Fantome screaming inside "I will catch you, little kids. MWAHAHAHA!" and then the portal closed, with his last words (or so we thought).

***

"First, they came to the hotel health room to meet me. Mom and Dad were so happy, meeting me." How are you, honey? Are you fine?" Mom said, in care of me." I'm fine" I replied," Where's Fantôme?" she said." He's in that portal you dreamed of. We locked him up in there. But, I have a feeling that he's gonna return. So we have to arm up". Matt said, as if he was a soldier (which he truly was for saving mom and dad)." We have to shift out of here, since Fantôme knows we are here. Or else, we're going to be in big trouble." Carlos said. He was right, but I was feeling too weak to move around." But how will we go somewhere else. We've got no transport and no money." Matt said. He really did have a point." Let me take care of that" Carlos said and he went off on his adventure while we went to the hotel health room.

***

Carlos went to "Vehicle Street" at once. Carlos had come here before and he was pretty sure he was going towards the right direction. At first, he didn't see anyone so, he thought he took a wrong turn or something, but then the clouds started to clear up. Carlos saw all the vehicles and people there .He went to one of the models to check it out. At first he didn't recognize it. But then he remembered it. It was the…"Ford Mustang model X!" he exclaimed, with joy." It's a beauty to look at, don't you think." a man said. He must be an employee there. Carlos got to know this because his name was written on a tag. His name was John. He was pretty good-looking and smart for his job." What can I rent for about…$100 ?I want a car for a week." Carlos asked, looking at the money in his pocket." You could get a… small sedan." John said. Carlos was disgusted because at a head count, they were 5 people. He asked for something a bit better for 5 people. John looked around here and there, and then finally pointed at a caravan. He said that someone had just cancelled a caravan and could lend Carlos it for a week, at a deal of a steal! He took Carlos to the caravan and he was impressed. But once he saw the inside, he almost fainted. He thought the inside view was stunning and couldn't believe that this was the employees' 'steal of a deal'.

Carlos agreed and John handed over the keys, while he handed over the money of a week to him. He told Carlos all the basic information, like airbags, GPS, etc (which Carlos knew already, as he read plenty of car papers) and key features of the caravan.

Carlos drove the Caravan as fast as he could to the health room of the hotel. As soon as he stepped inside the health room, everyone was staring at him. It felt very weird, but when he saw the clock, he figured out the reason. By the three moons, he'd been out for about an hour!" I have parked the caravan outside. Let's get going." he said to everybody, rushing inside the room." Great job, man! Wait a second, did I hear you 'parked a caravan'?" Matt said, while doing our handshake." Yeah, and you'll never guess which caravan I rented. The big RECREATIONAL VEHICLE one." he said, with a hint of enthusiasm in his body.

He sat on the chair beside me, relaxed. He turned my head to see Matt, but he wasn't there where he saw him last. Suddenly there was a voice up ahead of him saying" Come on guys, what are we waiting for, Fantôme to catch us? Let's get the heck out of here." It was Matt, jumping as enthusiastic as a monkey seeing a huge stack of bananas! We all went outside, and got in the caravan.

Everyone was surprised. There were two beds on the top, two convertible couches, small bedroom with queen bed, kitchenette with sink, a centre table with a pot of flowers on it, a washroom with a shower, and two seats ahead for the driver and the passenger in the caravan.

In the caravan, we were all silent. Thinking about where Fantôme could be. Just as I was about to say to everybody to not worry about Fantôme, the RV went over something big and jumped. Carlos squealed the brakes, shaken up from the jump. We all got out of the RV, to see what the object was that Carlos went over.

***

At first we thought it was Fantôme, by seeing it. But actually, it was more terrifying than anything we've ever seen. It was a kind of an army of duplicate Fantômes. But, once it screamed a huge army came from behind the trees, the bushes, the ground anywhere you could imagine. There were varieties of dummies. Such as skeletons, zombies, pirates and other ugly monsters you couldn't even imagine in your dreams." Oh, come on. I've been driving so far away from the hotel, yet they still manage to find us!." said Carlos, taking some objects out from below the back couch.

It was a baseball bat. What a perfect thing to carry at a time like this. He took out a sack of baseballs from the same place." GO. HIDE. I'LL TAKE CARE OF THESE LITTLE MONSTERS!" He said to us. I couldn't let him behind, and it looks like neither can my brother." We're not going anywhere without you." Matt and I said at the same time. We both looked in the same place and found some extra bats. Carlos was hitting everybody who were far away, while me and my brother were hitting anybody who came close." Thanks guys. You know, for helping me." Carlos said in a panting voice. He fell down in exhaustion, I went down to him and told Matt to handle how much he can. My mother took my bat from me and said "Take care of him, we can handle it.", while hitting the mannequins." Sit in the caravan, me and Matt can handle them." I assured him. Just as I was about to put him in the caravan, there was a loud honk coming from the car. It was coming backwards, I had to warn my family." Incoming car!" I shouted in a warning voice to them. They both jumped out of the way, while the Caravan hit the other Mannequins. I was stunned to see my father in the car, laughing his head off!" How did you like my rescue plan?!" he asked." Terrifying, but awesome" Carlos said, in a cheerful voice. The dummies were all dropped down on the ground.

We quickly got inside the Caravan and sped off at full speed, leaving the dummies behind. Now time to figure out where to go next. I have a 0% idea of where dad is taking us. There's a growling in my stomach, so I asked dad if we could stop at some fast-food place or something. An hour later we arrived at McBonalds. We all went inside and I got a happy meal and a Big Mack burger followed by a oreo Mcdrully for me, while the others got Big Macks, Koce and French Fries. We went back in the Caravan and munched down the food like a pack of werewolves. We each shared everything, and I took a few fries from them. After we finished, we threw everything in a dumpster can.

We were just about to start driving, but we started questioning each other about where we were about to go." We couldn't just keep on driving without knowing where we're going. We have got to have one final location!" Carlos said. I whispered to Matt that why does Carlos have all the brains, but he just shrugged and looked up for some places on Carlos's phone. There were many theme parks, water parks (We didn't have any swimsuits with us), cool gaming arcades (Matt and Carlos were the only ones interested in it) and SHOPPING MALLS! (Me and mom went crazy for that one). We had been living in the same clothes as day one even though it's been almost a week since we got here, because Fantôme stole all our stuff.

We headed for the Mall near us in an instant. When we reached there, we found out there were things that each and everyone liked. My brother and Carlos went to the Arcade Zone, mom and me went to Zax! for clothes and my dad, well, he was just roaming around. He had no place to go, so he just tagged along with the boys to the arcade. We also made a deal. While Matt, Carlos and dad were gaming, me and mom will shop clothes for them too.

It's a win-win for everyone, well everyone except dad. We played a lot of games, but Matt was the only one who made a high score.

The game Matt high-scored was" Boots of Thunder!". It was a dancing game where you had to move your feet as fast as you can on the tiles that light up. The high score before was 5008, and Matt made 5800! What a big difference I made. As dealed, we all went to the Turkish cones on the top floor at 2:00 pm. After a few minutes, me and mom appeared before us." Hey, we didn't know which flavour you'd like, so we waited for you!" I said, with my arms folded so I could look like I'm mad at them." Sorry, but I'd like Chocolate in a cone, we got stuck at the billing counter. Big line." I replied, taking out shirts and jeans and other clothes for us. Me and Carlos's eyes popped out by seeing the heap of clothes. It was like a miniature Mt. Everest!

***

They went to the changing room in the mall and we changed into the clothes me and mom got them. They was stunning. Fashion was written all over them. Matt was wearing an army track pant along with a shirt with guns on it, there was "ARMY COMMANDER" written on top of my T-shirt and finally, to top it off, an army denim jacket. Carlos wore denim jeans with a" Gamers Mode On" T-shirt, while dad wore the same thing as me. They were probably thinking of an Father-Son match for us. Me and dad were looking at each other as if we both were meeting for the first time and still wearing the same clothes. Then, we decided to go to Disneyland! Everyone was super-excited. We started the journey to the land of Magic & Fun.

CHAPTER 6

We took almost 1 hour to reach Disneyland from the "Swap Meet Americana Plaza" place. Normally, it would've taken half an hour, but with the traffic it took more time. We parked the Caravan outside the park. We went inside and Matt said" Quick, mom take a picture of me with mickey mouse!". Mom couldn't refuse the cute scene, so she took a photo instantly. But he shouldn't have said so, because when I was in line and it took a while for her to come ahead, mom lost her patience and started clicking photos of whoever was ahead. And that is the classic original photo-craze of mom. Also the reason why half of our albums are filled with pictures of random people.

After that, we went on some rides and did some photo sessions on the backgrounds there. Mom took plenty of pics, even though we insisted not to." It'll help in the photo albums we're gonna make once we get home!" she kept on saying to us, even though we knew she wasn't gonna. Once we go on trips, mom likes to show her friends and our relatives where we keep on going for trips through her social media accounts. We kept roaming around just to decide about which ride to go to. There were just so many that we couldn't decide what to do. Dad bought Matt, me and Carlos some cotton candy and some popcorn! We started with a fun-family train ride, which took us through some sets of imaginary lands. It made us totally forget about the Mannequin army. It was super-exciting when we went on that one ride where we were in the cart and it was just going in loops and zig-zags. We went for a ride called 'Jungle Cruise', where it was a boat going through wonderful artificial Jungle sceneries. It was full of different species of some cute while dangerous plants and animals (Also artificial)! There were mascots roaming around everywhere, for the childrens' amusement.

We were roaming around and saw a 'Haunted Mansion' ride. We explored the Haunted Mansion. It was just like 'Haunted Haven' ! I said" I love this, we made a good decision coming here. I-" Suddenly, I froze when I saw the sight in front of me. It was one of the mannequins that attacked us on park 32 lane street. I thought it was just part of the Haunted Mansion, but why would it be so specific to us and looking exactly like the army we encountered on 32 lane street.

"Guys, look who's coming up towards us!" I cried, pointing at the mannequin. We all ran for our lives, instead of enjoying all the wonders at Disneyland. We escaped to the backside of wonder falls, hoping that the mannequins won't see us." How did they come? I thought they were finished once dad knocked them off!" I said, pacing around here and there." I don't know, but we have to escape. Again!" Carlos said in a bored voice." Ok guys, I suggest that we just go back home. At least we'll be safe there." I said, in a voice which said 'Just agree, guys!'. Which we were not going to do at all." If we go home, what are we going to do. Get bored-to-death due to that "Drama Queen" Abby." I whispered to Matt, in a secretive manner." Stop being over-dramatic. Everything's gonna be fine, don't worry!" Matt said to me, in an assuring and relaxing voice." Yeah, yeah. You always say that. IT'S SOOO IMPORTANT!"I said, in a sarcastic voice. Before I could say anything, Carlos cut the conversation off.

"Guys, just stop fighting now. We have to find a safe place for us to hide and stay." He said, in a long voice that told us to really stop fighting. The fighting reminded mom and dad of our childhood." Oh look how cute they are, just like how they were when they were child." Mom said, just before clicking a photo of me, Matt and Carlos.

"Mom please stop it!" I said in a kind-of begging voice.

"Ok ok." Mom said, snapping one last photo of us.

"Come on guys, we still have to explore the different places." Carlos said, moving ahead of us." And die by those army of mannequins due to YOUR curiosity!? " I said" Matt come on, please talk some sense into him.".

Matt looked at the both of them, and then finally went next to Carlos." I'm sorry, but this time I'm on Carlos's boat of ideas." He said once he reached Carlos's side. I couldn't believe him. But, it looked like Carlos's decision was right. Because, soon enough, even mom and dad joined him alongside Matt. They all looked at me, raising their eyebrows at me in a startling way." Fine fine. I'll come with you guys, but just stop looking at me in that creeps way!" They all laughed, and then we started to go to our next destination. Without worrying about the mannequins behind us.

***

We couldn't really decide where to go next, so we made a list of dos and don'ts" Come on, you can't deny that we NEED to go to the Hot Wheels toy mall. Right, guys?" Matt said, looking at everybody as if it was a necessity to have it. As if we were going to die without it, well, he was going to die without it!" Nah guys." Carlos chimed in." It's more important to go to the musical store, where we could all play the instruments. I say we rent them and play them for a month or so." He finished with a crazy imaginary guitar solo which convinced others not to go to the musical store at all, especially Matt who was about to join Carlos's idea. Mom chimed in with her own idea.

"What if we go to the best place." She said, with a huge capacity of enthusiasm on her face." And what place would that be?" Dad asked in a full-on curious way." The grocery store!" Mom exclaimed, with happiness on her face and dancing in her mind." Not at all! That's the most boring place in the whole world." Everyone said at the same time, looking at each other in disgust and surprisement." Then where else are we supposed to go?" Mom asked in sympathy to all." How about…we do something wholesome! Like going to the library." Mom exclaimed, looking pretty excited. I was on board with that, cause I love books. My brother calls me a bookaholic for that reason. Me, Carlos & Matt agreed, although Matt didn't seem as excited as me and Carlos.

We went to the most friendly library in that whole town, which was closest to us. The" Little bookworm" library is probably the best library which I've gone to in my whole world. It had every single book I could even think of. To mention a few, there were Percy Jackson, Geronimo Stilton, Thea Stilton & autobiographies on the best footballers, cricketers, and scientists of the world. I took a korean book about BLACKPINK, which Matt hates. Dad took a book about psychology, 'cause he likes that sort of thing. And my mom took a book of a old-time novels. She says she likes to learn about the past-time history. Typical mom. Dad payed for the books and we went to the Caravan to read the books. "We're way far away from Fantôme, so let's just relax for a while. "Carlos said, laying down in the backseat where he comfortably made himself a bed from the neck pillows and the spare blankets. We were surprised and shocked to hear that from Carlos, since he was the one who wanted to rush up so that Fantôme wouldn't catch up. We didn't dare to mention that up to Carlos since he would start panicking then, so we decided to take the advice from him and started relaxing. "Man, it's been such a long time since we took a break like this! "Matt said in relaxation, flipping a page of his book. He was right, we'd been worrying so much that we forgot to take a break while travelling.

While relaxing, it felt like heaven. It couldn't be compared to anything in the world. Suddenly, a noise came from the below of the car. I thought that Dad accidentally hit the accelerating pedal for a second. But when I asked dad, he didn't know what I was talking about at all. So, he went outside the Caravan and a lot of grunting and groaning noises came from the outside of the car. I was too scared to look out, so I just stayed inside the car. Without knowing what was going on outside.

***

Dad came inside with mud and leaves on his shirt and face. I asked what had happened outside, and he replied to me" Ahh… there was some stick or rock under the tyre and the tyre deflated. So I had to replace it with the spare tyre instead, which took a lot of work." Dad said ending with a puff. And by the way he puffed with effort, it wasn't hard to believe that he worked REALLY hard." Okay everyone, get up get up. We have to start moving now!" Dad said with a hand gesture of getting up. "Why now? We've got plenty of time left, or is it that Fantômes' spies have come." Mom asked in a questioning voice." It's not that, we've got to go to the petrol station. We're low on petrol." Dad said checking the petrol box, and then showing it to mom. It was actually pretty low, which explains why dad is in a hurry. The caravan was drinking up the petrol like a whale bursting water from it's blowhole." Plus" Matt added with a hyper eye" We could eat something there.".

"Don't you think we've eaten plenty of food till now, you're gonna start the world hunger with your mouth. "I said, trying to tease him. But Matt didn't understand that, he was taking it seriously. "Well, not my fault that I'm always hungry. "Matt shot back at me with an angry face and gleaming eyes. We argued back and forth for a long time, until mom had to stop us. She said we were fighting like sewer rats who fought for food, which was actually enough to shut us up surprisingly.

We went to the gas station and Matt raced to the snacks shop faster than Usain Bolt, the fastest runner in the world. Matt looked around and started picking out packets of chips, sodas and other snacks. But mom told him to put it back to their places. We were all bored and dad told us that he was gonna fill the petrol to the top and it was going to take plenty of time, so we distracted each of ourselves with something.

We started moving as soon as everyone was done doing everything. Dad took pretty much a while to fill the petrol, more than expected actually, so Carlos, me and Matt started entertaining ourselves by playing hand games, truth or dare, etc." Ok guys, what should we do." Carlos said. Dad started thinking about it and suggested" How about visiting some fun place, but it will take at least couple of hours drive so you guys can sleep for a while.". Matt agreed and replied "Yeah, we've been just roaming around. I think it's better to rest. "I was shocked to hear that from Matt, but I was in no mood to sleep. "I am not going to sleep at all, I've had enough nightmares in this trip" I thought, with a face of horror. But eventually, I think I fell asleep after a period of time. When I woke up, dad yawned and announced" Okay kiddos, looks like you have to get out of the Caravan now for some fresh air.". I started to think that my dad was a maniac, since it has only been, like, 5 minutes or so." Dad it's been only been a few minutes since we got in the car. "I said with confusion in my mind. "OH no…It's almost been couple of hours since I've been driving. "Dad said stretching his back and Besides" mom exclaimed "I saw a board and it says there are multiple parks here!".

We hopped out of the Caravan like small kids ready to go to their favourite shop. What we didn't actually know was what we had awaited in front of us.

CHAPTER 7

Once we got out, we started exploring the different parks, and in one area there was an illusion park. We started roaming around and there were plenty of illusions everywhere. Carlos jumped into one and cramped his leg. We went on and on around the park, amazed by the illusions. We went around the central area where plenty of stalls were arranged. We all had some Twisters, which was kind of twisted potato on a stick with different spice flavours, and it was the most amazing thing I had ever ate in my entire life. Mom was getting some clothes and we sat on the bench beside. Suddenly, Carlos got up and went to the statue in the centre. We hadn't noticed the statue and we all freaked when we saw it. It was a statue of Fantôme, which was a bit hard to believe. I thought I was hallucinating a bit or so, because Fantôme's existence in this world is zero as no one knows who he is. Then suddenly, we remembered that this was an illusion park and we were probably hallucinating. The statue started to move and I thought it was Fantôme for sure, acting as a statue and then wanting to kill us. So, before the statue could do anything, I punched it in the head and we hid behind the nearest tree we could find. Oh come on, what are the odds of us running in the same people again and again. We all ran away, but me, Matt and Carlos got separated from mom and dad. We kept on running with Fantôme behind us. Suddenly, there was a staircase. Unfortunate to us, it was just an illusion and, we all fell face flat. We all ran faster than before, probably thinking that we were lightning. There was another set of stairs and we weren't going to be fooled again so we divided. Matt and Carlos went on either side of the stairs and I went through it. And just to my darn luck, it was an actual pair of stairs this time. Matt murmured to Carlos as I tumbled through the stairs, "That must have hurt." I finally got to my feet and Fantôme caught up with Matt and Carlos. They ran leaving me behind, but I sprinted through the stairs and overtook Fantôme. Once we got tired, we stopped. We would probably be able to fend off Fantôme because, it's three-on-one. Fantôme approached us and grinned. But actually, the coincidence was, it wasn't Fantôme! It was someone who looked just like Fantôme, but instead it was the nicer version of it. We heard it say"

That stupid little no-brainer Fantôme! He's left me alone all this time, and he doesn't even care to visit me once. When I meet him, I'm gonna punch his face with all my might, and then we'll see who's the one crying." It sounded like he was furious. No doubt he was mad at Fantôme, after all he's done to him. Suddenly, he faced towards us and asked who we were. We asked him why he cared about us and he said he saw us with Fantôme. We said that we were trying to hide away from Fantôme, and he laughed! He said that we shouldn't worry about Fantôme, and we asked why he did. So, in a silence and angry voice he said," I am Fantôme's brother". In a surprising manner by hearing this news, Carlos fainted. We tried to wake him up, but he was out cold. So, we decided to start listening to, as you could call him, Fantôme's twin. He said his name was Kaion, and then he started his story.

He was happy when Fantôme and he were created. They were the best of the best brothers. But then, it all changed when they were playing one day and Fantôme fell down a cliff. Kaion ran down as fast as he could, and saw some kind of tall wizard picking Fantôme up and running away. Fantôme couldn't do anything to protect himself, as his head had plenty of strings coming out.

But just as Kaion approached the woods down below, Fantôme disappeared along with the wizard. Once he had finished, I guessed that Kaion would say that they never saw each other ever again, and he did. But then came the twist. A few months later Kaion was roaming around in this same spot of the garden, and he saw some figure in the woods. It took him a while to figure out that the figure standing there was actually Fantôme. He was so relieved by seeing this, that he jumped up and bounced straight to Fantôme. But once he reached Fantôme he noticed something was wrong with him. He wasn't the same as before, with that sweet, sweet voice and that hand-shaking hand. Instead he was like a new model, or perhaps the same person, but only with a different soul. Kaion tried to talk to Fantôme, but he just got ignored by him. And instead of talking to him, Fantôme painted him gold and cursed him to stand like a statue forever. And if he moves away from this park, he will kill him! We took him with us, and if Fantôme came to actually kill him, we would be ready with some plan. We decided to trust him, but from a far distance, because we've learnt our lesson of trusting strangers. Especially dummies. We went down through some streets there and tried to find some place to stay. While dad was driving, we all chatted a bit with Kaion.

He told us about Fantôme and himself with us. And pretty soon, after knowing all his information, we were ready in case he betrayed us," Where are some places where Fantôme could hide, perhaps under a mountain or so." Matt said, with me staring at him for him thinking about something smart like this, and then sarcastically clapping." Stop teasing him, Lizy.

He's finally thought of something smart!" Dad joked with a laugh. Matt just ignored dad and said to Kaion" This information could be very helpful if we want to take revenge on him.", he said while looking at the weapons we had. And the way he said it, shook me up in a serious manner." Well there is this one place where Fantôme could've gone." Kaion said after a pause of recalling. We asked him about the location and he said that it was a mountain on the far-side of the local coastal beach under a rock-slide cliff. The name of the place was 'Coveside Cliff'. Dad said that we were close to the local coastal beach, and that he could change routes for a while. So, we decided to go there.

***

It took us a little longer than expected due to the traffic. I mean like it's a sunday, who wouldn't go to the beach. Once we reached the far-side of the beach, we started to look for the rock-slided cliff. Since this cliff was discovered by the dummies decades ago, there was a whole lot of natural development which had occurred from then. But there were no clues of Fantome being in that area." It could've been that I predicted the future. Because there aren't any traces or so." Kaion said, with a scramble on his and our minds. So, we planned to go ahead, but we just didn't know where to go, as usual.

Matt suggested that we should travel like one of those 'choose your adventures' books. Dad agreed because he was tired of looking at the google maps on the screen. So, on the first turn, we kids voted to turn right. And on the next turn the parents decided to turn left. Then after the bridge we just decided to go straight, and that was probably the best decision we must've made in my whole life. Because after that turn, we ended up in a small mall in the village called 'Luxburg'. Throughout the journey Kaion kept on blabbering meaningless things. In fact, many times he kept on irritating us and did not let us choose our destination.

Once we entered the mall, we found the best & most amazing waffle shop in the world. The waiter who served us was pretty kind and soft-talking. We enjoyed a lot because Kaion was in the Caravan and we were all alone. The reason why he's in the Caravan is because he was babbling a lot, so we decided to shut him down and keep him in the car. We left the mall and we went to the farm beside us, as we came to know that there are lot of domestic animals there. Just as we were all enjoying the milking of cows, Carlos remembered that a dummy like Kaion couldn't stay shut down for more than an hour, and he had been in the Caravan for at least 2 hours. We all rushed back to the Caravan in lightning speed. And surely enough, Kaion was up trying to break the glass to come out and have fun with us. But what he didn't know was that this was laminated safety glass, which was the safest type of glass and hardest to break. We came just in time to stop this. Dad sent Carlos to get some rope from the hardware store right beside us so that if required we can simply tie Kaion up whenever we can't take him with us or control his blabbering. It was almost night. Just around 7:00 o'clock. Dad searched up the nearest hotel and it was just around, an hour away from here. Carlos took out his headphones and started to listen to some songs." Which song are you listening to?" Matt asked him." Talking to the moon- by Bruno Mars "he replied.

"Can I listen to it a bit?"

"Sure, why not!"

Matt listened for about half a minute or so and then gave the headphones back to Carlos. Carlos went back to listening to his songs. Meanwhile, Kaion started blabbing around tearing apart our ears. Eventually, he started talking so loud that it attracted the police around us. Before dad rolled down the the window, me and Matt stuffed Kaion, who was blabbing, under the seats in the bag. Dad rolled down the window, and started talking to the police. They said that they heard some weird and loud noises coming from our car. Dad said that it might be the kids, "You know, kids these days. Always making some noises and having fun." dad said, in a nervous voice. The policemen looked at each other, then they looked at the car, and then finally shrugged and agreed with dad and went off in their own car. Dad let out a huge sigh of relief, putting his hand on his forehead to wipe out the sweat from stress. Carlos didn't even know what was going on, so while dad drove ahead, we explained the police incident to him. At least he heard something amusing tonight.

***

We reached the hotel and dad booked a room for us. He booked 2 rooms, both of which were deluxe rooms. One of them was for mom & dad, while the other one was for Me, Matt & Carlos. Carlos was so tired that as soon as he freshened up, he fell out cold on the pull out sofa which I made for him. Matt and I decided to check out on our parents. And I guess they were even more tired than Carlos, because they didn't even change their clothes and they were knocked out cold on the bed. We both decided to go to the vending machine with some of the spare change which we had. We were hungry anyways so we took some bottles of cold drinks, and a few packets of chips for everyone. Matt and I both started munching our packets of chips and reading our books. After that, we slept in a while. And once again, I thought I had a vision, predicting from the previous one. But this time, it was just a plain old dream of my family.

***

The next morning, when we got ready and went to the dining hall, I told everyone our plan which I created overnight. First, we all carry home-made weapons with us and be ready for anything. Next, once we stop at some location and they activate their master plan, we attack. And then finally, we imprison them in a place where they can't do anything.

Once we got in the Caravan, we were all silent. Except for Kaion. He said "Look guys, I don't think you all still trust me. So, I have a surprise for you. So, let's go to some nice place!". In the caravan, he gave dad the directions we needed to get to the canyon resort. So, dad started driving and we reached almost in an hour.

Once we reached, Kaion led us somewhere in a hurry. We acted like we were very suspicious and didn't know where he was leading us at all. We were just about to take our weapons out when Kaion amazed us by giving a surprise party! When we entered the dining hall, the room was filled with balloons and banners and celebration confetti all over the place. "Thank you for giving me a place to stay, for taking care of me. And for that I'm giving you this party as a reward. Thank you and congratulations!" Kaion said in a graceful voice. We all settled down our weapons and we were dumbfounded by this twist. We didn't know what to say to Kaion. We were all too stunned. So, we all sat down on a table and were all bewildered. Suddenly there was a loud thud and a high-pitched shriek. We all got up to see what had happened.

PART II

THE TWIST

CHAPTER 8

Turns out that while Fantôme was making his entrance, he fell on Kaion's head." What are you doing here, you idiot." Fantôme barked angrily." I'm just giving a party to my beloved caretakers, you absent-minded fool!" Kaion replied, rubbing his head in an affectionate way. And then pretty soon, it turned into a full-fledged fight. Me and the rest of us tried to escape as stealthily as possible, but we still got caught." Don't you dare try to sneak away, you little pesky mice."Fantôme shrieked from behind. And that's when I lost it. I don't know what exactly happened next, but all I remember is that I was punching and hitting Fantôme with my fists right into his stomach. Matt and Carlos were cheering on me from behind, while Kaion was screaming me to stop. Finally, mom and dad came to pull me back. And just when I held his hands loose, Fantôme laid his first right on my nose. I pulled back myself swiftly, holding my bleeding nose with a tissue paper. Fantôme got up from the floor, dusting his leather coat. Then in a deep and hoarse voice he bellowed "DO YOU KNOW WHO I REALLY AM! DO YOU KNOW WHO YOU ARE STANDING IN FRONT OF! DO YOU KNOW WHAT POWERS I BEHOLD AND WHAT I CAN DO TO YOU! PEOPLE LIKE YOU ARE LIKE TINY, LITTLE INSECTS IN FRONT OF ME! I WARNED YOU IN THE BEGINNING TO NOT COME IN MY WAY, BUT YOU JUST DON'T LISTEN.NOW, I GUESS YOU'LL HAVE TO LEARN IT THE HARD WAY." He started to say some weird spells, and Kaion immediately indicated us with his eyes to move away, probably because he had the knowledge of what spells Fantôme was chanting. We decided to just back away and get in the car. But just as we were about to step outside ... Fantôme shut down. Carlos appeared behind him and said" We'd forgotten that we could shut down these little menaces." We quickly scooped up Kaion and got out of there. Kaion said in an unsure voice "Look guys, I just saved you from that idiot. Do You now believe that I'm still on your side?". We all agreed to him and dad unlocked the car. While we were running, Carlos said" We've got to attack him sometime. This is enough, it's like he's torturing us in our minds." We couldn't deny it, we had to attack and we would really love it." We will, man's promise.' Dad said, once everybody seated in the car. Swiftly, Kaion spoke up and said" Uhmmm…Just wanted you to know, like I get shut down for 1 hour, Fantôme only gets shut down for 15 minutes.". By the name of chronos, how can this trip be more worse. And just then BOOM…Fantôme was on the windshield of our car! Dad swerved the Caravan left and right, and then he finally went on top speed and slammed his foot on the brakes which made Fantôme fly away. Dad accelerated the Caravan as fast as he could to go over Fantôme. But with Fantôme's luck, he rolled aside in the nick of time" YEAH RUN AWAY, YOU PESKY WEAK HUMANS!" He screamed from behind, once again brushing his coat. I think that Fantôme has sent a clear message now. He wants war! And if he wanted it really badly, I was ready to give it to him.

***

We reached our destination in the nick of time. We found a motel within our budget and decided to stay there. But let me just say, the quality was horrible! When we reached the room, the bedsheet had plenty of holes and scratches, the floor had scratches on it and the whole room was stinking. Mom asked if they had a better room, but the receptionist said that this was the only one we could get within our budget. Mom returned and said that we would have to manage here. We locked Kaion in the closet and started making our arrangements. We pulled out the sofa-bed for me and Carlos, while Matt was supposed to sleep with mom and dad. But Matt said that he can sleep alone and when we asked him how, he gathered all the pillows and cushions from the sofa, aligned it in a bed-like shape and slept on it. We slept and I had another vision.

***

I was on the mountainside cliff on the far-side of the local-coastal beach again, but this time, I was the one listening to Fantôme and Kaions' conversation." I think that the family's on me" Kaion said to Fantôme in a kind of raspy voice." Of course, they're on you, you're MY twin. And anyways, they're not a dumb family." Fantôme said in an irritated voice.

"Yeah yeah, I'm sorry.So what's our plan, the one you signalled me with on my voice modulator.

Then, it looked like Kaion was about to say something else, but he took a pause and instead said" Wait… somebody's watching us. I can sense it." Fantôme started to look around, so I thought that this was the perfect time to escape. I moved from there and BOOM…I was back in reality. I woke up, soaked up with sweat and looking around. Only Matt was there, sleeping soundly like a koala. I decided to go to mom and dad to tell them about the coveside resort trap. On my way there, I saw some kids playing around and I thought" Who could be playing here right now at midnight!?".

I decided to see it on my way to mom and dads room. One of them were just about to crash into me, so I said to him in an angry voice" Slow down a bit, you'll get hurt.". I guess my 'scolding' shook them up a bit. Because the next thing I knew was that the kid was calling his parents in their room. So I decided that it would be best if I rushed to mom and dads room. And right before the parent opened the door, I burst open in mom and dads room. First, they were scolding me about what could be more important than sleep. And I told them about the cove side resort trap and told them that we were right about Kaion and he was dangerous, just like his brother. Suddenly, I realised something. Kaion was missing from the bed. He thinks that I don't know a single thing about him knowing that I've spied on them. Well, I guess it's time to spoil his party now, because that's what he did to our vacation. I told my parents everything and my plan, so we immediately rushed to the car with Matt and Carlos. We raced, as fast as we could, and finally reached coveside cliff. We finally found the cliff and the mountain, but Fantôme wasn't there. We were confused about that. It felt a bit suspicious, so we decided to send Carlos to spy. Once Carlos saw Kaion, he went and hid behind the dome-shaped door-like rocky figure. He spied on him from an average distance and heard and saw everything. Once he reached, the voices he heard were Fantôme and Kaion." Have you got their trust." said Fantôme

"Oh, I've got it all right. It'll be like them falling into a pool of piranhas once we're ready." replied Kaion. Suddenly, there was a loud noise of chanting in the background. Turns out that Fantôme's army was right behind them, chanting in a huge voice. Fantôme raised his hand and the chanting silenced." You haven't got it completely." Fantôme said" And since you are my brother, you won't get it easily. I can assure you of that for sure.", he then let out a sigh. Carlos accidentally knocked over a few rocks and the twins looked at his direction, but they couldn't see him. Carlos thought to leave right then, but he needed to stay. Everybody paused for a moment or so, then Fantôme and Kaion continued. Just as Kaion turned around to approach us, Fantôme called out to him "My brother, remember, Grak Tung ! ", and then the whole army called out "Grak Tung !".Carlos realised that now was the time to move, and he sprinted on to us. Once he reached us in the line, Carlos told us about the whole thing and that we were right about Kaion. We asked him why he had come puffing and running. And he replied that he had gotten stuck in the rocks, and that there was a possible chance that they saw him. Kaion came outside a moment later. But till then, we were all gone. Kaion returned back to the motel, and we all pretended we had gone to sleep. He adjusted himself in the same position of how he was when we put him in the cupboard, before him leaving for Coveside cliff.

***

When we went to the breakfast buffet, we discussed a bit of today's plan (Without Kaion, of course) and Matt asked when we would be going back home. Dad replied to him" As soon as we get our revenge on that 'menacing little fool' kiddo.".

Matt understood what dad said and ate silently. We ate devilled eggs, some bread toast and a bit of cereal along with the snacks we had for breakfast. "Well, if we're on VACATION with a 'devil' chasing us, we still are on vacation. So…let's go to the beach today. "Mom said in an enthusiastic voice. All of us cheered at mom and agreed happily. Matt packed his goodie pack for the beach and we joyfully took Kaion out of the cupboard for the travel. It took us a few hours to reach the local beach but once we reached, we changed to our swimsuits and went in the water. After swimming in the water, me, Carlos and Matt made a HUGE sand castle, which was pretty fun!

Then once that was done, dad got some ice-cream for all of us. We licked it up within two minutes and it was super-tasty! We stayed at the beach till lunchtime and then left with a free sandwich in all of our hands. Once we got in the car, we took votes of where to go next. Matt voted for the arcade, me and Carlos voted for the library, and mom and dad voted to go to the theatre.

But, before we finalise our next stop we all agreed to go for lunch. Dad looked up some restaurants on the web and we all decided to go to a waffle-shop named 'Belgiumm bites co.'. And it looks like that was the best waffle-shop in the world, because it's 'chocolate-vanilla waffle' was the best! In fact, it was so good, that I ordered a second one. Once we left that place, we decided to check the carnival going on around the corner of the town. There were plenty of rides in the carnival. Like the ferris wheel, ball toss, and whatever else you can see at a carnival. We went through the stalls and there was a ventriloquist dummy at one stall, so we sped up there and learned more about dummies. They also told us a couple of their secrets which they had learned about dummies, but none of their secrets were helping us with how to destroy our 'special' type of dummies. We left the place, empty-handed. But Matt did get a free toy, which he ended up breaking in a blink of an eye.'

There was one place which had this awesome snack called 'Butter On A Stick', which tasted like heaven. Mom said that it contained too much butter and fats and whatsoever, but once she tasted it, she regretted her saying. In fact, she loved it so much that she took a second! Once that was done, we roamed around the carnival for a bit and went ahead in the car. But when we reached the car, Kaion was GONE! The door was open, which gave us the hint of how he escaped. We didn't know exactly how he opened the door, but with small legs like those, he couldn't have gone far. So, we started searching the places around. And since this town is so small that we could go around it within 30 minutes. All of us started searching in different areas of this town. Dad rented a double-seat bike for Matt and Carlos. I also got a bike, and mom and dad went in the car. Dad bought us all compasses and walkie-talkies. Our plan was that Matt and Carlos cover up the whole north area of the town, I will cover up the whole east area, and mom and dad will cover up the south and west area. I was roaming around with the compass in my hand, when suddenly I saw an injured-looking creature. I was scared to death about what that could be. I ignored my fear and stepped ahead.

***

I was in mixed feelings of fear and confusion. The fear was that the 'injured-looking creature' could be Fantôme or Kaion, while the confusion is that the creature could actually be an injured animal. I stepped up ahead, making my decision to go and catch whatever it was. And to my luck, it was Kaion, who had broken his head in Fantôme's fall. I quickly scooped him up again and ran in the direction of my bike. I signalled to my family from the walkie-talkie, "I've caught Kaion, guys! Come meet me in our Caravan as fast as you can.". I joyfully sat on my bike, put Kaion on my bike-carrier, sped up ahead. Once I finally reached my car, I plopped Kaion in the backseat, buckled him up and locked the door." Now what? Where should we go next, guys!" Matt said in an enthusiastic voice. Almost as if he had eaten some gluten pancakes!" Matt, did you eat any gluten pancakes!?" I asked him in a mysterious voice. He replied no, but Carlos spoke up and said that he bought it for him because he had requested for it. Matt gave a scowl and elbowed him in the side-ribs after that reply. And that's when Carlos realised that he probably shouldn't have said that." Oh honey!" Mom said in a reasonable voice" You know that you're allergic to gluten. Then why did you still eat it?". Matt held up his hands as if he were surrendering to a crime and said" Yeah, I know. I'm sorry!" I explained to Carlos that he's kind of allergic to gluten, because when he eats gluten, he gets all hyper. He promised that he would be cautious next time. The apology was ok, so I told Matt to take his medicine immediately. Matt complained that he didn't like his medicine, but I told him he had to. While he took the medicine, I went over to dad. He looked at the car from all the sides and announced that we were going to take a quick relief-break (He says that when he wants everybody to calm down and let him do his work in a relaxing way), and he was going to do a few repairs to the car. He considered about the future war with the twins, and wanted to make sure that the caravan was all set and ready to go for it. He started pumping the tyres and I helped him do the job. He appreciated my helping and sent me off to bring some lubricating oil to fix the tyres. I figured out my way on the streets pretty much by then, and it was even more fun since I was riding the bike. Once I came back, I saw Carlos had started fixing the hood of the car, which was pretty much impressive. I asked him how he could do it and he replied that he had taken a course on cars a few years ago, when he was 12. I moved ahead and gave dad the lubricating oil. He then instructed me on how to lubricate the tyres, and sent me off. I didn't quite understand it much, so I went to Carlos for help. He showed me how to unscrew the tyre, how to oil it properly, and how to screw it on again. He instructed everything on one tyre and I did the other three. Once the job was done, I showed it to Carlos. "Not bad at all for a beginner! Such a good and impressive job. He appreciated me. I thanked him and went forward to dad. He thanked me and I screwed them back to the car. Dad was impressed with all of this and he asked me how I did all of this. I answered to him by pointing a finger to Carlos and said" He taught me it all.". Dad went over to Carlos and said" Thank you for helping out my daughter, kiddo." Thank you, sir. I appreciate it, but don't ever call me a 'kiddo'." Carlos said, smiling and patting dad as if he and dad were old mates. Dad shook his shoulder in disagreement of Carlos' manners.

CHAPTER 9

We started driving for Coveside Resort as it would be the location where we would mostly find Fantôme. It's almost been, like about… 2 weeks! I calculated the days and I got 10 days! I wasn't sure about it, so I asked Carlos to count the days from when he met us, and he replied 10 days. We're supposed to be home in 4 days, and we're stuck in this Dummy Catastrophe! Dad came back and I said to him "Dad, our 'official vacation' ends in 2 days, and we're just roaming around like crazy! Plus, I've got plenty of essays in English, history, and physics to do.". I was probably freaking out a little bit like an overdramatic nerd, but I couldn't help it because I'm the topper in class and I've got to keep it that way in every test. Dad told me that 1 test won't make such a difference in the class, but yes … it would make a huge difference. Some part of my brain told me to calm down and I agreed to dad. I forgot all about the essays and went to plan along with Matt and Carlos. We had to do something and we decided to make a plan. But before, we shut down Kaion, so that he couldn't hear anything about our plan to destroy them. Matt said with a grin "Why don't we start a nuclear war on them!". Carlos snickered at the idea. I sighed "You don't start a nuclear war on dummies the size of a pillow, you dumbo!". But he just kept on laughing. I started on doing some calculations, and then we finally got the idea. We planned on making a chart of them based on their weaknesses and strengths. Here's how it turned out: Kaion had a weakness of his brother being hurt. While Fantôme had no weakness, or we haven't found it out yet. But Kaion has the strength of manipulating someone with his own things. While Fantôme had the best power of being strong and smart, which helped him make a devious plan for Kaion to follow.

We tried to drive as fast as we could to the Coveside resort, but our fastest was just 30-45 minutes. We searched all over the place for Fantôme, but we couldn't find him at all. Finally, after 15-20 minutes of back-bending, we left the place empty-handed. But, once we got in the car, we saw something in the bushes moving. Then suddenly, it stopped and there was a loud BUMP! on the rear end of the car. We ignored it and drove ahead, but then we heard footsteps on the roof of the car. Once we reached the road there was a smack on the windshield of the car. Turns out that the figure in the bushes was actually Fantôme. We all screamed at the top of our lungs and dad swerved from left to right to shake Fantôme off. Finally, dad slammed on the brakes, which sent Fantôme flying ahead. Dad drove right over him and Fantôme screamed for his life. Kaion couldn't bear looking at this and took his seatbelt off & jumped out of the car, running to Fantômes' aid." You'll regret this, you dirty rodents." Kaion screamed at reaching Fantôme, but it didn't look like he was sorry for Fantôme. It looked like he was laughing a bit. Dad sped up the Caravan and we went to the market. Because we were about to go to war.

***

We reached the market and picked up anything we could find that looked like it was a weapon or could combine it to anything that could make it a weapon. We took some duct tape, scissors, a box of screws, clear tape, a hammer, a cooking knife, a bag, some tsar bamboo from the farmers market, and a notebook with some pens. None of us understood what dad wanted to do with all of that, but he said that he had a great plan to attack Fantôme and that he would explain it to us and that we just had to remain patient.

We took all the materials and went in the Caravan so that dad could explain his 'masterplan' to us. He took the notebook out of the bag along with the pens and gave one to us each. He then drew a dot on the paper in the middle, which he said indicated Fantôme. Before dad could continue, Matt said" What are we gonna eat for dinner guys! It's almost 6:00!". He was right, and our tummies were grumbling a bit." We'll look at that later, first, listen to my plan." dad grumbled in his anger voice. He explained to us how the Tsar bamboo is the strongest bamboo in the world, which could help us knock Fantôme on the head. Dad took out the notebook and started to explain how we would attack on Fantôme with our 'Weapons'! We started to leave when I got a call from someone. "Well, look who decided to call right now! Abby Summer." I said in a sarcastic voice. Matt groaned at the name of 'Abby Summer'. "Abby's a pretty nice girl. "dad said.

"Well, she might be nice in front of you, but she's torturous in front of us. "Matt said in a wide-eyed look, pointing at me and him, continuously. Dad shrugged, and signalled me to pick up the call from Abby. I picked it up and put it on speaker. "Hello Abby, what did you call for?" I asked, as if I wanted to cut the call immediately.

"Oh, Hi! Just wanted to check on you and how your trip is going on."

"Well, glad you called, cause the trip's going amazing."

"Okay, I just wanted you to ask if I should pick up the mail from your mailbox, because it was getting so full that the mailman couldn't put any more in it."

"Yeah, sure. Was that all you called for?!"

"Yeah, plus I was thinking that I could ride your bike while you're away, I won't damage it at all. I promise!"

"Okay, but keep it back where it is once you're done riding it. Bye!", I said in a hurry and just was about to cut the call. Abby spoke up "But, wait, haven't you heard about the incident. Someone tried to break into your house. Or at least, as I think, tried to break down your house."

We were all dumbfounded, even Carlos! And we cut the call without saying another word. Everybody stared at the phone, but I diverted them back in the plan.

We all packed up the weapons and stuffed them in the car. As dad was driving along the road, he stopped in front of a perfectly good trash can, got out of the Caravan and put the trash-can in the trunk of the Caravan where everything else was. Then, he drove to an alley and we all got out. Dad told us to find anything we could to fit ourselves, such as metal figures or anything else. Then he carved a hole through the metal trash-can with the knife, and made Matt wear it. He knocked the hammer on the trash can and Matt didn't feel a thing. Dad showed this as an example and told us to find something like this. He said that if we couldn't find anything our size, we could bring it for someone else in our group. I found a Halloween costume that fit me and a cloth bag. Carlos found some metal scraps which fit my costume and another trash-can. Mom found some flattened stones and a broom. Dad told us that we three kids would attack for the plan and they both would be the back-up plan. Matt and Carlos would be in the metal trash-can. While dad would apply the metal scraps on my Halloween costume with the duct-tape. And since the cans were looking old, dad went to the shop around the corner and bought some blue and red paint to colour the cans. Carlos painted his red and Matt painted his blue, since he insisted it." Great job, everyone! Now, let's discuss our plan." Dad said to us, with his serious face on." This feels like that one final plan in Nascar when the captain of Norwegia needed to win the cup!" Matt jumped in, literally! We all rolled our eyes and we all started by putting our suggestions for the plan. And soon enough, we were pretty impressed by our plan. And we were ready to put it into action.

***

Once we were done making all the armouries, we started practising on how we would fight with Fantôme. We all wore our armours and dad threw stones and whatever he could find at us, while we had to defend. We did that for plenty of while. At first, nobody got the hang of it. But after 15-20 minutes, we started to understand it. Once we mastered one, dad started throwing 2, then 3, then 4, and then multiples at a time. After a few hours, we got the hang of defending and started testing each other out. Dad gave us a small break and we started attacking after that. I attacked Matt, while Carlos attacked me. Then, it was just vice-versa. Once we got good with attacking, mom and dad started a tournament between us. First, it was Matt against me. But the challenge was that dad and mom would throw some rocks at me and Matt, and we had to defend or dodge them while attacking. And the hardest part was that, in the middle of the match, Carlos would start attacking and whoever he attacks, would have to fight both as there were two of them. Fantôme and Kaion! I was having a pretty smooth start in the fight when it was time for the unleashing of Carlos to happen. I fell down on my knees while dodging Carlos, and I was hurt on the knees.

But my dad kept on encouraging me to fight. I knew that in the real fight I would have to keep on fighting. So, I slid him down on his knees and sat on his back and pinned him to the ground. Dad whistled and screamed" Carlos, OUT! Matt, gotta beat Lizy out to win! Lizy, excellent pin down. You gotta stay the winner!", which kept everyone motivating. Well, everyone except Carlos, that is. In the rage of motivation, I accidentally hit Matt on the chest hard. He collapsed to the ground, holding his chest part on the trash-can, coughing. I felt really bad and crouched to his aid. But as soon as I reached him, he stopped moving. I shaked him as hard as I could to wake him up, but he wasn't moving at all. Suddenly, he woke up and threw and pinned me to the ground." Haha, sucker… LOL! Pranked you at last. "Matt said pointing at me, still laughing like crazy. "You should've seen the look on your face. And look who was calling me a monkey. "Matt muttered to me out of his laughing voice. Dad pointed to Matt and said" Hey…no pranks buddy. It wasn't funny at all. You're disqualified.". "Proud of you honey, I knew you were a strong fighter. "Mom clapped at me and held my hand up like a referee holding the winners hand up. Dad looked at us and felt proud looking at his new warriors which he made." Hey, why don't you try with me Mr. Morris. I'm sure it could be fun!" Carlos asked dad, holding his hand out. "You sure bro. He used to work in the army. "Matt said, trying to make Carlos change his decision. Carlos nodded since he was ready for it." Fine, but I'll put a challenge for you. Matt, I'll put you in charge. Your mission is that you have to protect Lizy before me or mom puts a tape on her. While you and Carlos have to protect me or mom from tagging her and she has to stay there standing. "Dad said, commanding us like a proper sergeant.

Carlos and Matt were doing their best to protect me, but suddenly dad swooped in between, almost touching me. But Carlos saved the touch at the last second, becoming a hero." I'm going in, Matt. Protect Lizy safely."

Carlos said to Matt, swooping and running to dad in his direction. He was running around and Carlos couldn't see him anywhere, but suddenly dad appeared from behind the trees and Carlos slid behind dad and tripped him down." Great job, man.

But you failed the mission. Anna already got to Lizy." Dad said in his push-up position. They both ran down to our base, where I had a tape on her arm.

CHAPTER 10

"What happened? I thought you were on Lizy's' guard, Matt." Carlos said, pushing Matt on the chest. "I told you not to go after dad, but you didn't listen. "Matt said to Carlos, in anger. The argue lasted long enough, until dad separated them apart." What were you thinking of, Matt. Letting Carlos go away and leaving you all alone with Lizy! I'm very disappointed in you. ZERO MARKS!" Dad scolded Matt in a ferocious voice." Actually, sir." Carlos spoke in "It was my fault, since I made that decision myself. I was in a good chase…"Carlos stopped with dad speaking up. "Chasing what?! Individual glory?!" Dad finished with an angry voice. "Let this be a lesson for you. All of you. "Dad stomped off, angrily. I was going after him, but mom stopped me." Don't. Let him be alone for a while. It'll make him feel good. "She said, and I sat down calmly.

We were all bored and started reading. Carlos took out his book and started reading it. He was reading the'

Mythology of dragons', which was about dragons maybe. We asked what it was exactly about, and he said it was about some 'Destiny Dragons' and what more. Matt was so uninterested that he fell asleep in the middle of the story, and it was bedtime now. So, we decided to go to bed (A.K. A the caravan). And once again, I thought it was time for another nightmare. But to my surprise, for once, I had a nice, restful sleep. But as soon as I woke up in the middle of the night to drink some water, I saw Matt sleep-walking. He does that oftenly, but I stopped him before he could go any further and put him back in bed. I read my book a bit in the Caravan light. While I was reading, Carlos woke up. "What happened. "he mumbled to me in a sleepy voice, rubbing his eyes while trying to wake up.

"Nothing, just couldn't sleep. Have to keep an eye on Matt so that he wouldn't sleepwalk away."

"That's funny. I remember when I used to sleepwalk in my elementary school. "Carlos laughed.

We laughed and talked until we slept away in our beds.

***

I woke up to the sounds of the Caravan door's opening and my family pushing against each other. At last, I couldn't hold it and woke up. Carlos was already up and dressed, while Matt was just brushing his teeth. My hair was all curled and looking like a bird's nest. Mom was making breakfast with the leftover snacks which we had in the grocery bags which we had Bought. My mother is always fond of cooking, and she makes the craziest things out of any item she can find. And to everyone's surprise, it always tastes the best. We told her to take part in some cooking competition at some, but she just won't do it. Today she made some oats custard with melted bubble-gum and skittles on top. Along with a side of some sweet and chilli chips, which are my favourite. And, believe it or not but, she made all of this by only using one-third of our items. We weren't pretty enthusiastic about this meal, but again she can make some pretty good items with minimised items. We asked her why make it out of less items when we have more. She said she wanted to save it for the after-time, which we didn't understand. Probably something like a mom saving thing. We tasted the oats custard and, it tasted like heaven!

Once breakfast was done, dad executed today's plan for us. We would all start searching for the Dump Korf (Which is 'dummy' in German and our secret code) in different directions at a time. First, we headed North, the common direction to start on, and stopped at certain suspicious or well-known places. Such as the gas stations or any forests. Next we went East, but still we got no luck. Then we went in the direction South, and thought that we found something in the bushes. But it turns out that it was just a raccoon waiting for the apples to fall out from the trees after giving a hard push to it. We stayed there for a while to watch the raccoons' entertainment. We left and headed in the last direction left, West. While driving on the road, to our luck we finally found Fantôme and Kaion going for the sewage. Dad slammed on the brakes before hitting the two maniacs. We let them go through the sewage, quietly observing. They went in the sewage as expected." Bro, they didn't see us at all. Those dummies!" Carlos laughed. I suspected that they did see us, but didn't react at all. So that they could be focused on their plan. Suddenly, there was a huge light coming from under the sewage entrance. We then figured out that they were carrying a torch. I widened my eyes with realisation…" Dad. Drive away!" I screamed" They're gonna blow it up!". Without asking any questions, dad drove back and almost crashed the wall. Just as we reached the dead end, the sewage bombed up.

***

The explosion cost a toppling of a car on the way. Fantôme poked his head out, unharmed, and cursed at us with his brother by his side. Although we were surprised and shocked to see them unharmed, at this moment. We didn't pay much attention to them, and attempted to go right over them. But they just ducked right into the sewer, and we almost toppled over by the huge gap between the road and the sewer. Fantôme and Kaion saw this as the perfect opportunity to run away, as we were down. Dad ordered me, Matt and Carlos to go after them and mom and him would stay here. We all unbuckled our seatbelts and ran after the two douchey dumpkorfs. We saw them taking a right turn from the central street and headed in that direction. We saw a crossroad and were confused. We finally decided that I would go to the left path, and Matt and Carlos would go on the right path. I passed by a few houses which looked haunted because of the old oak trees in their yards. I wasn't that happy with this path, but I was the one who chose it, so I had to suck it up. I didn't know if there were any dangers here, but it would be better than Matt and Carlos having it. I hoped that any second now, I would find a trash-can. Yeah, yeah, the request seems a bit…. no, a lot weird, but it would come in handy for, you know, trapping the dumpkorfs. I didn't see any trash-can, but I did find a stick to my luck. I was ready and prepared for anything that would try and come in my path, but just a minute later, Fantôme attacked me. Not to mention it was a surprise, but he caught me a bit off-guard. But with the skills which I remembered from the day of the training, I rolled Fantôme over to the ground. "Why are you doing this? What will you ever gain from it? Why are you torturing us? You could just leave us alone and mind your own business!" I said to him, while banging his head against the streets. Fantôme laughed raspily and replied" Slavery! I want to rule the world, and you will help me, Lizy Morris.". All of a sudden, I realised that Kaion wasn't here." Where is he? Your no-brainer twin, Kaion" I grumbled with a loud voice. "I had an instinct that you'd choose left." Fantôme said to me" So I sent him to the right. It, of course, will be a pleasure to battle with you.". I reported to Carlos through the walkie-talkie" Carlos, code red, code red! It's a snatch. Report back to base. And don't forget to bring the no-brainer." He confirmed and I took off to catch the running-Fantôme. He started dodging my catches and throwing anything he could find to throw as a obstacle in my way. He wasn't an easy target to catch. I knew that if I left him, he would find us under any circumstances. And I didn't want him to harm any other families. He started kicking down trash cans and things so on, just to make me trip. So, at least I got one of my reasons right. That is, he is dumb as a rock. Finally, I somehow managed to get a hold of him. I started making my journey back to the car, and tried my best to save my ears from bleeding from his intensified blabbing. As soon as I reached, I told dad to stick Fantôme somewhere where we can keep an eye on him. Soon Carlos and Matt came behind me panting. With Kaion in their hands, they both said" What do we have to do to these Dumpkorfs now." My dad took some duct tape and pulled out a bunch." Let's tape these twins to their positions."

He said pointing to the trunk seat of the car. Fantôme yelled" You'll never get hold of us and keep us hostage! You'll never...", we taped him before he could say anything more. We taped them both right in front of our sights so that they couldn't escape us again, And we drove off to a secret area. Dad was driving for plenty of hours, and we decided to do some different things in it. We had done plenty of activities in the other trips, and we couldn't figure out what to do now. We tried to identify new ones, but the best activity we found was hitting Fantôme and Kaion with the tennis ball we had. We had actually found the game by accident. Matt was just playing with his tennis ball when he accidentally hit it on Fantôme. Fantôme felt that was really annoying and he let us know it by the look on his face.

We thought that it was probably better for both of us so we kept on hitting him. I mean, he did deserve it after all he had done to us. And plus, it was so exciting that even mom wanted to take a chance. Kaion was just sitting there quietly, which just wasn't right. Because, compared to his brother's fussing, he was less fussy and more intelligent. I told Matt to check on behind of Kaion, and I made him do pretty much the safest thing. Why? Simple, it was because Kaion was trying to cut his rope and as soon as he saw this, he told Carlos to stop him and Carlos tied a new rope upon him. He even tied another layer of rope on Fantôme, you know, in case he also tried to cut open his rope, again. We all slept because we were pretty much tired of all the fighting and running and all, even though it was just 11:30 a.m. We all woke up around 1:00, which was also time for lunch. But we weren't that hungry. So, the ones who were a bit hungry just ate a few of our snacks. And consisting them were Carlos and, as usual, Matt. He can never stand without eating anything when it is available with him. Me, dad and mom started making a plan for the 'Grandè attack'. We wanted to just go home and give up, but dad said that we needed to finish those little maniacs. We didn't know how to get rid of them. Surprisingly they always survived all our attacks, from one during the escape of parents, then car accidents, party fight and later Sewage blast. For sure, There is some secret around their survival and we were not aware of it, but we did know somebody who probably did. We drove back to horror park's resort. It took us most of the day but once we reached, I should say that it was definitely worth it. As soon as we reached, we entered and stomped off to our mysterious old pal, Larry!

***

When we first saw him, we were all in the reaction to kill him, since he knows about Fantôme (And, possibly, his 'twin'). And just by the reaction of us, he spoke up to say "You all want to kill me, right!", in a sheepish manner. And these were the two answers which we got from our 'receptionist'.

A. He did know one weakness about Fantôme

B. He had not have a single clue about Kaion

The weakness was type of rare and it was extremely hard to defeat him in. The weakness was that he could only be killed in his birth place, and only with fire. He then looked around here and there, and whispered to us that they're birthplace was the point of mysteriousness (The 'Mysteriousness' part was just for us), Good 'ol Coveside Cliff." Well," Matt sighed "That's wasted a lot of money and materials in our lives." He pointed to the stash of notebooks, pens and the other items we picked up from the store. "Okay, we have no need to practise now for the attack." Dad said "But is there any room available here, Larry? We really need to crash here for the night.", he looked at Larry in a convincing way. Larry started calculating about the rates for a night here, but dad stopped. Larry agreed and thought about it for a while as a second decision, and then replied "As long as you don't leak my secret about…" He took a pause, looked around and then whispered "You know what…...!"

We agreed and Carlos went to fetch Fantôme and Kaion, while we all went to the rooms assigned to us. And thank goodness, it was on a lower floor this time. And by lower floor, I mean the 8th floor, which we were pretty much okay with as long as we got a place to even stay. "Okay everybody" Dad said" We'll spend the night here today. Then go for breakfast first thing tomorrow, and then we'll leave for the Santa Monica beach for the coastal rocky cliff." He finished off with a yawn, and, before you could even say 'Paprika!', he hit the hay. And from dads' last words, I remembered a famous saying from the god of poetry, Apollo, 'Know yourself, and nothing in excess.' (I learnt it in history class).I thought that as a pretty logical thought for ignoring the information about Fantôme and Kaion. But then again, if I had to stop them from wreaking havoc anywhere, especially to us, I had to complete the attack. Only then I could go home without fear and filled with pride. Soon enough, there was a loud knock on the door just when I was about to leave for our room. It was Carlos, holding Fantôme and Kaion in his hands. "Where should I keep these two?" He said and held them down the mattress of the couch to prevent any noise from them. "We still haven't figured out where to keep them." I yawned at Carlos "I'm thinking that we could keep time-shifting posts to look out on them.". Carlos thought about it and volunteered for the first shift before I could even think about it. But, I was pretty much tired from the day that I let him have it. I told him that we'll be the only ones taking shifts because Matt and mom and dad were all sound asleep. He said that he would give me my shift around midnight and I nodded, and dozed off beside Matt. I was pretty much sound asleep when I heard a loud CRASH! at the edge of the hallway. I woke up and checked the time.11:45, Almost time for my shift! Suddenly, I heard another crash at the edge of the hallway. It sounded like wood was banging against wood. I got up, just to see that Carlos was gone from his chair. And so were Fantôme and Kaion! I went out of the room to check on the scene outside, and I found Carlos struggling to recapture Fantôme and Kaion. I, immediately, went into the room. I came back to him in my 'Aquatic Animals!' nighties and my kitty-cat flip-flops, holding a pillow bag in my hands. I signalled Carlos with the pillow cover in my hands to hold down the maniacal twins inside with. He nodded and I counted down to three with my fingers, and unleashed the power of pillow-kidnapping on Fantôme and Kaion."Looks like you've got a new way of telling me that my shift has started!" I panted at Carlos. He nervously laughed and focused on holding the maniacal twins down, not replying at me. We took the pillow cover towards the room, and threw it inside the closet. Carlos told me that he'll stay a bit extra time, because he took a bit of my time in the 'maniacal twins' issue'. I said that it was okay, but he insisted on it, so I let him have it.

I went back to sleep, but only this time when I woke up, it was time for breakfast. I was a bit confused because I don't remember taking my shift at night. But that's when I realised that Carlos let me sleep in and safely secured the twins in the closet. I got up and went to Carlos, who was sleeping on the chair where he was watching the twins. I shook him by his shoulder and he woke up in a startled manner (Which I couldn't blame him for as anybody would be startled to wake up from a deep and incomplete sleep). He looked at me like a complete stranger and then rubbed his eyes as if he didn't know who I even was! Then he spoke up" Oh hey, how was last night for you?". I punched him in the shoulder and he said" Oww! Why'd you do that?", I replied to him "Why didn't you wake me up for my shift?". He said that he tried to wake me up twice, but I didn't wake up. So, he kept the shift to himself. I couldn't believe that I overslept, but actually I could, because I am quite a sleeper. Before I could argue anymore with him, dad said that we had to get going for breakfast, so I had to freshen up quick. I brushed my teeth and took a quick and tiny shower. By the time I came out, they all left. Well, everybody except for Carlos because he was still tying his shoelaces. "OH, they've all left and are just… down the hallway." he said, looking just outside the door. I quickly took out my sports shoes and started tying them. As soon as I was done, me and Carlos sprinted down the hallway and rushed right into the buffet! We scanned the area and saw my family sitting on a table. We both filled our plates with the yummy Skeletal soup which was just Tom Kha soup with some bamboo canes inside them for hard skeletons, A puff-pastry which had a ghost design out of some powdered icing-sugar and a slice of some last night's frankenstein cake. We met up with my family and sat down with our filled plates." Hey guys, what are you all talking about ?" I asked them, and Matt joked to me they were talking about about my "Nuclear war" comment (Which he was laughing his head off about). Mom replied to me in a realistic way that they were talking about the plan for the coveside cliff attack. We quickly took some second servings, ate it all and hurried up to the room for Fantôme and Kaion. We scooped them up and they started singing, which could also be called shrieking, in our ears, extremely off-key. Like, seriously, they needed to take some singing classes. We threw them in the cars' backseat and gave them a nice double-knot tie." Where are you all taking us to, dummies! Oh wait, I know, to your funeral!" Fantôme laughed maniacally, and Kaion laughed along with him. And I think that because it was part of his kindergarten syllabus, HAHAHAHAHA! Hey it looks like I can joke pretty nice, too! Anyways, we were just about an hour away from the coveside cliff. And the best part is that, the maniacal twins didn't even know where we were heading to! Then the biggest worry possible at this time just came true. Fantôme asked where we were going, and we said…" None of your business, suckers!". We all felt so relieved after saying that, and so happy.

Carnival Of Horrors

CHAPTER 11

The rest of the trip was pretty much peaceful and it was now time for the final step. And that was… eating a hot-dog! We just felt like having one so that we could be a bit more prepared for the final step. We were supposed to be ready back then, but we just got a little nervous. After eating the hot-dog, we drove to the coveside cliff super fast. We picked up the maniacal twins and went for the long-ish hike to coveside cliff. It took us a bit longer than it did last time when we hiked here. Maybe it was because there was a large tree right smack in the middle of our route, grown and enchanted by the wizard! On our long hike, Fantôme was always trying to escape, but we wouldn't ever allow that. Dad held him so tight, that his escaping was probably impossible. Once we finally reached the cliff, we set Fantôme and Kaion down and, as expected, they tried to run away. Me and dad tripped them on their knees, and then punched them in the nose, just like Fantôme did to me. We picked them off the ground and threw them across the floor. Carlos and Matt also wanted to get onto this action, so they went over to the other side, and threw them to us. We played this game of catch-catch for a while, and then even mom wanted to join us. So, we kept her as the monkey in the middle. Whenever she got the dummies, she would give them to the one who threw them, again. This play went on for a while, until Fantôme caught balance and punched Carlos in the face. Then Fantôme run to the centre corner, which was far backside, and took out a fire torch out of the pile of stones. Kaion followed behind him and helped him create a fire out of the stones. Once it was ablaze, he commanded us "If you do not bow down to me, I will set this whole place on fire and even you! So, I wouldn't do anything stupid if I were you." with the same raspy voice, but more villainy inside it. Me, dad and mom all tried to approach a few steps ahead, but he gave us the threatening look of the fire burning the stones. Matt and Carlos scooted a bit front when they weren't looking, and I signalled them to take the torch out of his hand and burn him apart. He nodded at me and, after a while, he and Matt went into action. Matt had gone forward and held Kaion in his arms and tried to throw it at us, but it would've been of no use and he kept Kaion in his hands.

Seeing this, Fantôme tried to run away as far as he could, but with small feet like his, he couldn't run that fast.

Carlos immediately jumped out for him, but had a slight miss. Finally, when he came close enough to me, I leaped out and grabbed him by the knees. I banged his head by the ground and threw him across the room towards Kaion." Time for you to say goodbye, little maniac!" Carlos said." No!" Fantôme shrieked "I will live for revenge, my servants. Mwa-ha-ha!". We thought it was all over, but then his voice echoed in the cave "GRAK TUNG! GRAK TUNG!". The ground started to tremble and we started to hear some chanting "GRAK TUNG! GRAK TUNG!". I remembered something from my visions and said to the rest of the guys "This chant was in my vision. I remember. Just be aware guys, something big is coming!". Suddenly, the Mannequin army emerged from the rocks. Dad smirked "Looks like that all wasn't a waste of money after all, buddy!". We started using every single fighting skill we learned and dad started commentating again! With all the skills, it was pretty easy to withstand the Mannequin army. But yet, with all our skills, it was not easy for 5 of us to fight against an entire army of 100 Mannequins. Suddenly Carlos had a thought, he went behind and got a hold of Fantôme. We looked back. Carlos laughed in an uncertain manner and instantly set Fantôme ablaze. It took a few seconds for fire to spread upon him. Once Fantôme was completely destroyed, he vanished into dust inside the pile of rocks and surprisingly the entire Mannequin army also disappeared in a pile of dust and rocks, and we all clapped and cheered.

But then, Carlos scanned the ruins of Fantôme and then looked perplexed. Dad asked what was wrong and he said

"Kaion's missing.". We all looked around and he really was missing. "Let it be" Dad said "When he strikes back, we'll be ready and then we all left that place.

Carlos was standing outside, and dad asked "Why you standin' outside, buddy.". Carlos sighed and said in a deep voice "Well, I'm just a friend of yours. Not family." Dad laughed and replied in an enthusiastic voice "Are you kidding, you brought happiness to my boy when he had no friends. You made this 'boring' trip the most memorable trip for my kids, and without you, we couldn't have defeated Fantôme. You're more than welcome to call us your 'Family'." Carlos appreciated that, and then we all had a nice and big family hug. We all went into the Caravan after the hike. And, apparently, since Fantôme was destroyed, the humongous tree as also half destroyed. The other half was probably signalling of the living of Kaion. Dad started driving and he asked where to drop off Carlos. He said to drop him off at the same alley where we met for the first time. Dad went to the place and we all started playing different games. Since this was the last time we were seeing each other, we each gave our phone numbers to each other to stay in contact with each other.

***

Once we reached Horrorpark hotel, Carlos started packing his bag. Once we reached the final destination, Carlos got off. Dad asked him where his house was, and he said his house was the one just up the railing on the left side. He asked if anyone was living with him. And he replied that he was living alone, when dad asked why so he replied that his parents had died in the house fire when he was just 12, and that he was the only one who survived out of the house. He said that he works a part-time job along with his studies. We were all heartbroken upon hearing this. And from the reaction on dads' face, he wished he had regretted asking so. We all fell silent upon hearing this, but we still continued with our farewells. Then we told him that if he ever felt lonely, he as always welcome to come at our house. Mom shared our address on a page of the notepad and Carlos said that he would come for sure. Dad said "You're a pretty strong and independent boy for a 14 year old, and I appreciate everything you've done for us on this trip. Thank you!" He gave him a salute and we then watched Carlos climb up the stairs to his house and wave us goodbye. Then, dad started the engine and we drove off to our 'Home Sweet Home'. We all talked about how kind Carlos was when he helped us and time flied so fast that we reached just for dinner-time, but we decided that we'll just order some Out-N-In. Once we put foot in our neighbourhood, the first person we saw was Abby. And then all eyes were fixed on us, which was type of weird. Everyone started asking us questions all at the same time, but everyone stepped back when Abby came ahead. She started asking questions about our trip to us, but we said that we will answer everything tomorrow morning. We rushed to our house and slammed the door shut, immediately. But we saw a mail on our front porch, so we went outside and took it into our house." Who could've sent us a mail right now?" Dad said in a perplexed manner. It was an anonymous letter with no sender name or context. I ripped the mail open, and this is what it read "We will seek revenge and leave you restless, Little Servants!". The letter was confusing, but that's when I realised that the last thing that Fantôme called us was 'Little Servants'. I told everybody "Fantôme isn't completely destroyed, he wants to have revenge on us." Dad said" Impossible, he burned ablaze in front of us. But let me have a look at that letter first." He took the letter from my hand, squinted at the handwriting and said "Fantôme is destroyed for sure, but this is Larry's' handwriting. He and Kaion are working together to arise Fantôme again.". We were all confused, but it all made sense, since he was the one who knew how to destroy Fantôme. He was even confused when we wanted to talk about the 'Dummy in our closet'. He wanted to take Kaion, but since they're twins, he didn't notice the difference and took Fantôme instead. He wanted to work with Kaion instead of Fantôme, because he knew that it would be impossible to control Fantôme. That's why he told us how to destroy Fantôme and not Kaion. He took Kaion with him and hid somewhere. We all knew he must be there right now. So, we called the police and explained to them about Larry being a thug (Because they would obviously call us 'Bonkers' if we told them about the twins) and told them to arrest him. We told them the address of the coveside rocky cliff, and told them that was most probably the place he would be. They told us that they would look onto it, and we thanked them. Matt and I stepped out of the house, and went to play tag along with the others. We saw mom and dad sipping tea on the front lawn while talking to each other, laughing. We decided to play tag with Abby and the other kids in the neighbourhood. We came home after an hour so and freshened up. And luckily, till then the In-N-Out had come. We set up the plates on the sofa, and were just choosing what movie to watch when, the telephone rang.

I got up to see who it was and it was Carlos. Carlos just called to say that he was thinking about coming at our house day after tomorrow, for the weekends. He said that he was getting a leave for the weekends and thought about spending it here. I told him that it was cool and that he could come whenever he felt like it. And just like that, he cut the call, thanking me. I went back in the hall to dad and said that Carlos would be visiting us in the weekends. He said that was excellent and we sat down to watch the movie.

***

"Hands up, Larry! Your crimes have been put to a stop." The police said, entering the coveside cliff with handcuffs in their hand. Larry put his hands up and dropped the flowers he was putting on Fantôme's statue.

While Kaion dropped dead beside the statue. Larry didn't know what to do and tried to run away. But the police tripped him, took his hands behind his back and handcuffed him to his back." No!" Larry screamed "You can't do this to me. I am innocent as a lamb." He kept staring at the lifeless and limpless body of Kaion. One of the policemen chuckled "We actually have every right to arrest you Mr. Larry Thurston." Larry started cursing at them rapidly in latin and pointing at Kaion. The police ignored him and carried him out of the coveside cliff and put him in the police car. Then, suddenly, Kaion sat up straight and smirked "Habebimus Ultionum!".

EPILOGUE

CHAPTER 12

2 YEARS LATER

CREAK! The floorboard sounded when Fantôme set foot into 'California central jail'. He sneaked upon every cell to look for Larry. Suddenly, a policeman on guard passed by him, and he stood still like a statue. As soon as the guard passed by, Fantôme started sneaking upon the cells again. Finally, after 52 cells, he found Larry in a cell sleeping. His chin was covered with beard and he was very fat. He had a lot of hair everywhere, and was drooling and snoring. Fantôme squeezed through the metallic bars, just missing by an inch and, and slapped Larry hard on the face. WHAM! Larry woke up with his eyes widened and sat straight, scanning his cell. He saw Fantôme beside him and said "The heck are you doing here?". I've come to rescue your soul, you dummy." Fantôme smirked. "Wow!" Larry sarcastically exclaimed "Took you long enough.". Fantôme ignored his saying and continued "Now, Kaion is destroyed. But, he was just a pawn for us, and now we should begin with our real plan. No wonder his name's 'Dummy' and mine is 'Ghost'! Cause I am…Spooky!" grinned Fantôme, rubbing his wooden hands together. Larry got up and asked how they would escape, because he was too small to fit through the bars. Fantôme smirked and took out a toxic-like potion. He then poured the potion on the metallic bars and the bars dissolved into liquid. "Like this!" Fantôme chuckled, and they both escaped as fast as a cheetah running for a gazelle to the car, with policemen chasing behind them. The tall police gates stood tall like a warrior, but Fantôme dissolved that, too. Once they seated onto the Caravan outside the gate, Larry started the engine and they took off for their revenge. Mwa-ha-ha-ha!

TO BE CONTINUED . . .

FANTÔME HERE, READERS!

You actually thought that I was gone forever. Well, that was just my plan. Now that Kaion is gone, I will impersonate as Kaion and take his revenge. Leaving the Morris family restless! it'll be the perfect time to eat their brains, literally. HA-HA-HA. I am currently planning on how to destroy them to ashes. And don't worry, I'll come back with another spine-chilling, ghost bumping book for sure. Because I am, after all, Fantôme. Now, goodbye my dear fellow readers. And, trust me, the next will be spookific enough to wet your bed a year ha-ha-ha. Now I will go manipulate some more people. And, don't worry, you're next ! HA-H-HA!

www.ingramcontent.com/pod-product-compliance
Lightning Source LLC
LaVergne TN
LVHW061618070526
838199LV00078B/7332